The Body Builders

The Body Builders

A Novel

Albertine Clarke

BLOOMSBURY PUBLISHING
NEW YORK · LONDON · OXFORD · NEW DELHI · SYDNEY

BLOOMSBURY PUBLISHING
Bloomsbury Publishing Inc.

1359 Broadway, New York, NY 10018, USA
50 Bedford Square, London, WC1B 3DP, UK
Bloomsbury Publishing Ireland Limited,
29 Earlsfort Terrace, Dublin 2, D02 AY28, Ireland

BLOOMSBURY, BLOOMSBURY PUBLISHING and the Diana logo are trademarks of Bloomsbury Publishing Plc

First published in the United States 2026

Copyright © Albertine Clarke, 2026

All rights reserved. No part of this publication may be: i) reproduced or transmitted in any form, electronic or mechanical, including photocopying, recording, or by means of any information storage or retrieval system without prior permission in writing from the publishers; or ii) used or reproduced in any way for the training, development, or operation of artificial intelligence (AI) technologies, including generative AI technologies. The rights holders expressly reserve this publication from the text and data mining exception as per Article 4(3) of the Digital Single Market Directive (EU) 2019/790.

ISBN: HB: 978-1-63973-713-0; eBook: 978-1-63973-714-7

LIBRARY OF CONGRESS CATALOGING-IN-PUBLICATION
DATA IS AVAILABLE

2 4 6 8 10 9 7 5 3 1

Typeset by Westchester Publishing Services
Printed in the United States at Lakeside Book Company

To find out more about our authors and books visit www.bloomsbury.com
and sign up for our newsletters.

Bloomsbury books may be purchased for business or promotional use. For information on bulk purchases please contact Macmillan Corporate and Premium Sales Department at specialmarkets@macmillan.com.

For product safety–related questions contact productsafety@bloomsbury.com.

Part 1

Ada was twelve when her mother killed the dog. She was relieved when it died. It made her realize that life wasn't for everyone.

It was a golden retriever with soft curly hair. Her mother bought it after Ada's father moved out, to replace him. She named it Faustus. It quickly became clear there was something wrong with him. He sat beneath the radiator in the kitchen and barked all night, from when Ada's mother turned out the lights to when she came back downstairs in the morning. Whenever anybody tried to touch him, he shook as if he was terrified. But he was always trying to be touched, and he suffered from incessant digestive issues. If he was left alone, he ate everything he had access to—edible or otherwise—and then hid in shame beneath Ada's bed.

Ada's mother decided that he was jealous. She turned the space under the stairs into a miniature version of their living room, with a green velvet sofa meant for children and a small Persian rug. On the wall she stuck printouts of the same art reproductions that hung over the fireplace. It was fenced in by a baby gate. For one night Faustus was happy and didn't bark.

"All he needed," Ada's mother said, "was to feel included."

Two days later a builder came to repair a crack in the ceiling. Faustus ate a tube of ceiling glue left in his tool kit and ran out the open front door into the bright, sunny street. He was found three days later by a friend of Ada's mother, running along the concrete path above the pebbled beach. He had apparently not stopped running the entire time. The pads of his feet were worn down to bloody open sores. Ada's mother told her he had been sent away to live with a couple she had met in line at the pharmacy.

When Ada heard the news, she knew that the dog was dead, and she knew that her mother had killed it out of pity, because both of them knew that he shouldn't have to suffer by living in torment. A few years later she passed a woman with a golden retriever on a leash who strained towards her as if in recognition, but even though the dogs looked exactly alike, she knew they weren't the same.

ADA HAD A secret that she had never told anyone. There were things she knew that she should have had no way of knowing. Sometimes a voice spoke to her and told her things that she knew to be true by the way they fit in with what was happening around her. It told her that her mother had killed the dog. It didn't tell her how it had happened, just that it had. It made sense because Ada knew her mother couldn't bear it that the dog was always suffering.

"He's soaked up all the misery in the house," her mother said, "like a sponge. But he doesn't know how to get rid of it."

Ada thought she was wrong. Faustus had been unhappy before he had reached them. There was something wrong with him: he was defective, as if he'd been manufactured incorrectly. One time Ada had tried to trim the curly hair that was always in his eyes. At the last second he had jerked away from her, and the scissors had left a long gash down the side of his face. He hadn't made a sound but had looked at her sideways so that she could see the white parts around his eyes, and afterwards he left the room whenever she came in. Ada was sure that he had done it on purpose.

Her mother was a lawyer, and her father was an IT technician. They had met at university in Leeds and moved to the countryside outside of Norwich when Ada was born. The house they lived in bordered the marshes, and in the summer they went swimming in the tidal inlets. Ada's mother swam every day, all year round. When the tides were inconvenient, she swam in water so shallow that the front of her body became covered in mud and silt. Sometimes her father took photographs of the rusty tin-roofed barn in the field next door. Several of these photographs hung on the wall in the kitchen, above the stove. He always photographed the barn at the same angle, but the distance from which he took the pictures varied.

When Ada was eleven, the voice told her that her parents were getting a divorce. She was sitting at the kitchen counter waiting for her mother to come home. At first she thought the voice had come out of the radio, but then she realized it was inside her head, as if somebody had put it there. It surprised her that she hadn't thought about her parents' marriage before. When she came home from school, the house was always empty. Her father spent all his time in the basement, and her mother came home after it was dark. Ada didn't know where her mother went, only that when she came back, she was cold and silent. The tips of her fingers would turn white, and then red as they warmed up. The only thing Ada could think of to explain it was that she had been standing alone on the beach, watching the ocean. That day on the way home from school Ada had seen her black coat flapping around her in the wind as she stared out at the rough gray water.

Ada didn't know what to do on her own in the house, apart from wait for somebody to come back. It always seemed too dark, even when she turned on all the lights, partly because the walls of the living room were painted a deep maroon. It was like everybody in the world had disappeared and she was the only one left. If her father took too long she would start to believe that she was disappearing as well. She was sitting very still in the kitchen, aware of her mother through the wall, facing away from her and across the blank sea. It was like she was a vacuum, an object in the shape of a person. She couldn't move. Then she heard the voice, and it was like a door swung open inside her head. Through it she could see a black tunnel, like a mine shaft, stretching down inside her. That night, she dreamt she saw her mother walk forwards into the water until she disappeared under the waves. Ada got up very early, before anyone else was awake, and found her mother's coat, stiff and wet, hanging over the edge of the bath.

The next day Ada fell down the stairs and broke her wrist on the stone paving of the hallway. There was nobody at home, and she waited on the cold floor, thinking about her mother. She wondered how loud she would have to scream for her mother to hear her, but she knew there was no noise she could make that would be loud enough, so she stayed silent. She didn't think to call her father, who would be on the way home. When he arrived, he found her lying in the same position she had fallen in. He asked her why she hadn't gotten up to call for help.

"I wanted someone to find me," she said.

"That's ridiculous," he said. "I don't understand." He drove her to the hospital without saying anything else.

From the top of the stairs it had looked like a red carpet extended all the way to the opposite side of the wall, sealing over the gap where the staircase had been, but when she stepped forwards there was nothing to support her. She spent the night in the hospital. Both of her parents stayed in the room. It was the last time that they were all together. When they got home,

Ada's father sat both of them down in the living room and told them that he was moving out. He left the same day. Ada remembered noticing that her wrist didn't hurt at all. Two days later her mother bought the dog, driving to Wales to pick it up from a breeder who told them that both of its parents were unusually sensitive and intelligent.

There was no reason for the voice not to be real. Ada imagined a satellite transmitting information directly into her head. Somebody must be responsible. As well as the voice, she had a lump in the back of her mouth, where her soft palate met the opening of her throat. She assumed it was some kind of implant. Her parents had never noticed it. Since whoever sent her the information knew so much about her, more than she knew about herself, she assumed that they were always watching her, wherever she went. They could see inside her head. Nothing was private. It was comforting to think that she was never alone. Although she waited for it, thinking something else would surely have to come, nothing more happened until she met Atticus.

THE FIRST TIME Ada saw Atticus, she only had to catch sight of the back of his head to know that a mistake had been made, and he was who she was really supposed to be.

She went down to the pool early in the morning most days. In the daytime it was full of children. Their parents stood around the water, talking to each other over the noise. They made Ada feel embarrassed, as if she were doing something wrong. She was excluded because she was alone. She imagined that if she got into the water one of the parents would come over and say, "Can't you see that the children are having fun?"

Now only Atticus was there. She noticed him when she came in because she had never seen him before, and she wondered if he was also new in the building. He was turned away from her, sitting upright on a lounger, so she only saw the back of his head. It was covered in gray curls, soft and matted like lamb's wool.

Her swimsuit was beneath her clothes, and she got quietly undressed in the corner. Although she walked past him on her way to the water, she didn't turn around. The white tiles of the floor were cracked. On her head was a pair of goggles. As she got into the water, she could feel that he was watching her. Climbing down the ladder, she imagined herself from his perspective, her flat, pale back descending into her blue swimsuit like a cliff into the sea, the soft ends of her wet hair wrapped around her shoulders. She swam a full length before coming up for air. When she turned around, she saw straight into his pebble eyes.

Looking into his face was just like looking in the mirror. It wasn't that they looked the same. She thought that he looked like an old greyhound. He had a long nose and sunken cheeks, and he was covered everywhere in freckles and moles. It was, rather, that when she looked at him she felt sure that she knew exactly who he was, and who he was was the same as who she was, as if they were two identical objects from the same manufacturer. Both of them were separate from other people. He left the pool while she was putting on her clothes over her wet swimsuit. He had his towel wrapped around his waist. His chest was broad and smooth. He hadn't gotten in the water. Ada thought he must have swum before she'd arrived, but she couldn't help wondering if he'd been waiting for her, to establish a connection.

SHE DIDN'T SEE him again for two weeks. Her cousin Francesca came to use the pool. Francesca was tall and thin with long blonde hair that fell limply around her face. She worked in marketing. When she had first moved to London, Ada had helped her paint the walls of her bedroom a deep red. After they were done it looked like the room was covered in blood, but Francesca said that was what she wanted. It made her pale skin look even paler. She laughed when Ada pointed it out.

"It's artistic," she said. "I'm an artistic person, and I need an artistic bedroom."

Atticus was beside the pool. Ada had known he would be. Francesca laid out her towel on the tiles instead of using one of the loungers. She chose a position directly in front of Atticus, facing him across the water. It occurred to Ada that he wouldn't be able to look at them if they used the loungers, as they were only on his side of the pool.

"That man's looking at us," Francesca said.

"Do you want to move?"

"No," she said. "It's fine." Atticus had the same colorful towel wrapped around his waist. He was reading a book. "People who do that are always posing," Francesca said.

"He'll hear you," Ada said. The smallest noises traveled the length of the pool.

"No, he won't," Francesca said. "Anyway, he should know that we know."

Both of them got undressed. Francesca was wearing a bikini the same color as her skin. On her head was a black turban that held her hair away from her broad forehead. There was a thin silver bracelet around her ankle.

Ada looked at Atticus. He was still reading. The night before, she had dreamed about him, but she couldn't remember what had happened, only that he was there. Francesca stretched herself out on her towel. Ada knew that Francesca wanted Atticus to look at her. It didn't matter who it was, but she couldn't bear to not be looked at. After a while she said that she wouldn't swim, because she didn't have enough time to shower and change before going to work.

"I'm going to be fired," she said. "But it's okay. I was too junior for the position anyway." She shifted on her towel so that she was lying on her front with her head on her pale arms. "It's relaxing just imagining getting in the water."

"Why are they going to fire you?"

"My boss is jealous because I'm more beautiful than her. Last time her fiancé came into the office she wasn't there, and he asked if he could take me out for lunch." Ada wondered if Francesca thought Atticus was watching her. She looked over at him to check that he wasn't. He was still reading his book. She knew that Francesca was making it up, and that she would never tell Ada the real reason she was being fired. Her noticing Atticus had sparked a small fire of competition. Abruptly Francesca sat up. "Your mother called me," she said. "She asked me if you were all right."

"I'm fine," Ada said.

"I know," Francesca said. "That's what I told her."

"Did you have lunch with him?"

"Who?"

"The fiancé."

"Of course I didn't. She should wear less lipstick. It's always on her teeth."

After a while Francesca gathered up her things and left. The heels of her shoes clicked loudly against the floor. Ada got in the pool, but she only swam two lengths before getting out again. When she was back on her towel, Atticus put his book down.

"You know the loungers are free," he said. He had an American accent. He had to speak loudly for her to hear him across the room. "You don't have to lie on the floor."

"I know," she said.

"Do you do it because it's good for your back?" He sat up. "My back always hurts. I worry I'll develop a crooked spine."

"You should lie on the floor," Ada said. "With a tennis ball under where the pain is."

"Will that help?" He swung his legs over the side of the lounger so that he was facing her. Ada felt that she had his complete attention. Her hair dripped chlorine-scented water down her back.

"It's what my father does."

"I spend all day at the computer," he said. "I'm a writer." He looked across the pool, then back at her. "You remind me of somebody."

"Who?"

"I don't know."

"Do you live here?"

"I'm staying in a friend's apartment. You might know him. Neil. He's lending me his apartment while I research a book."

"I don't think I've met him."

"Neil doesn't swim." Atticus sat with his hands clasped between his legs. On his thumb he wore a silver ring.

"I'm a writer too," Ada said.

"How lucky that we found each other." He played with the ring, twisting it around his finger. His face was serious. "Do you get lonely?" he asked.

Ada thought about it.

"No," she said.

"Of course not," Atticus said. "You have yourself." Behind him there was a sign that asked people not to dive because the pool wasn't deep enough. Ada imagined hitting her head against the bottom and splitting it open. She wondered how long it would take for the pool to turn red with blood.

"Everybody has themselves," she said.

"I don't know about that," Atticus said. He paused, looking at her. "Can I have your email address?"

"Yes," Ada said. Atticus got up from his lounger. He wasn't tall, but he stood up very straight. He walked around the pool to hand her his phone. She typed out her email address and handed it back.

"I'll send you a message," he said. "So you'll have mine as well. My name is Atticus. My father was Greek."

When she got upstairs, Ada looked at the email. It was a photograph of the corner of the pool, where the blue water met the white lip. He must have taken it before she came in, because she hadn't seen him do it. The caption read "the light is beautiful here." The window was open and she felt the breeze on her face. Her skin felt thin as tissue paper. Outside, the blue sky was filled with small white clouds.

THE NEXT MORNING the light that came through the window was still gray and weak when she opened the blinds. She wanted to see Atticus, and she knew that he would be there, waiting for her.

Ada had moved into the building because of the pool. It was unusual for London. Her apartment was a studio. On one side was a bed, and on the other was a kitchen, separated by a plastic countertop. Only the bathroom had a door. When she thought about the shifting blue water lying seven floors below, she felt calm. She loved going down the stairs, descending lower and lower in a tight spiral until she broke the glassy surface and the water closed over her head.

Atticus was there, as she'd known he would be.

"Ada," he said. She felt light when he spoke, like the cells that held her together were coming apart. She realized how rare it was that she heard anybody say her name. "I was hoping you'd come down." Again, he was sitting on a lounger. Ada realized that she'd never seen him swim.

"Why?"

"Because I missed you." He said it lightly, as if it would make her laugh, but afterwards he looked at her to see what she was thinking. She smiled. Instead of a towel he wore crumpled black trousers that looked like pajamas and a white shirt. "Are you sure we haven't met before?"

"I don't think so," Ada said. "I haven't met very many people." He looked down at the cracked tiles. Ada thought he seemed embarrassed. She wanted to tell him that she knew what he meant, that she was sure they were connected, but she found that she couldn't speak. There was something in the way, as if talking about it would make the truth vanish. The night before, she'd had a dream where she'd tried to put on her swimming costume, but it wouldn't fit. When she looked down at her body, she'd realized it was Atticus's body rather than her own.

"I have to go," he said. "I have to meet a friend. I've been here since five, just in case you came down early." He looked at her. "I have a lot of friends," he said. He stood up. As he passed her in the doorway, he took her hand and squeezed it. When he touched her, Ada thought she was going to disappear. Then he dropped her hand and vanished into the stairwell.

In the night he'd sent her another picture. It showed the sun rising over the flat brick rooftops outside his window. The building was on the top of a hill, and you could see all the way down the shuttered main street to the park, where the ground began to curve upwards again. In the early morning only the park and Ada's building caught the sunlight, leaving everything else in shadow.

Ada sat beside the pool but didn't get in the water. She tried to memorize every second she had spent with Atticus. Nobody had ever paid her as much attention. She remembered him looking at her while she swam. She was not used to being looked at. It was as if curtains had been drawn back to reveal a secret audience she hadn't realized she'd been performing for. The knowledge gave every action a new and secret meaning. Even a single observer meant that she was acting out her life instead of living it.

When she got back upstairs, she looked him up. His email address told her his surname. She didn't read the reviews and articles. There were a lot of pictures. One showed Atticus standing in front of a wooden house, the roof of which had partially fallen in. Behind him was a desert landscape littered with rocks. In the distance the narrow line of a mountain range was barely visible. Ada thought that he looked around her age. His curly hair hung down to his shoulders and he was wearing a white vest that made him look frail. Around his narrow shoulders hung a blanket patterned with colorful geometric shapes. He was looking off to the side, as if somebody had called his name. Another photo showed him leaning against the bonnet of a truck. He seemed more in proportion, less puffy around the face. There was a caption that read "the author as a young man." It was dated seventeen years before Ada was born.

Ada felt sure that she had seen these images before. The blanket he wore around his shoulders reminded her of a blanket her mother had owned, that she always draped across the back of the sofa. Her mother said that it was special, but Ada didn't know where she'd gotten it from. It was thick and heavy, more like a carpet than a blanket, and the pattern reminded Ada of the desert.

In her wardrobe was a box of pictures. They were taken by her father, and most of them showed Ada and her mother on the marshes behind their house. He said that he hated taking pictures inside because real life happened on the outside. Ada emptied the box onto her bed. There was one picture, she knew, of her in the living room, which her mother had taken. The blanket would be on the back of the sofa behind her. When she found it, she held it up against the picture of Atticus on her computer. It was exactly the same. The coincidence made her feel warm and excited.

She called her mother.

"Do you still have that blanket?" she asked.

"Which one?"

"It was always on the back of the sofa."

"I don't know what you mean," her mother said.

"I'm looking at a picture of it," Ada said. "It was colorful with that geometric pattern."

"I don't remember it," her mother said. "Maybe your father took it with him when he left. Why are you asking?"

"I want it," Ada said.

"That doesn't mean I have it," her mother said.

THE NEXT TIME Ada saw him wasn't at the pool. She was on her way to a shift at the restaurant, and there he was, sitting in a café. He was wearing a leather jacket. They saw each other at the same time. Ada turned to cross the street towards him and stepped into the path of a car. She heard the blast of the horn and realized it had nearly hit her. The pigeons pecking around her on the street flew up into the air in a gray volley. As she stepped backwards and waited for the car to pass, the driver shook his head disapprovingly. Ada wanted to reach in through the window and hit him. She was shaking and put her hands in her pockets to hide it.

Atticus was standing up beside a small, round table. There was nobody else on the street.

"Oh, my god," he said. They stood facing each other. He looked scared. His gray hair was disheveled. Deep bags hung beneath his red eyes. "I don't know what I would have done."

"It wasn't that close," Ada said.

She sat down at his table. A moment later, he sat down as well. On the table was an empty espresso cup. Spilled coffee made a brown ring around the base.

"I don't know how to explain this," he said, "but I feel like I've known you for a long time."

"I know," Ada said. For a while they sat in silence. Atticus seemed nervous. With one finger he traced the raised lip of the table. He looked at her, and then looked away again.

"I want to be around you all the time," he said.

Ada looked at him. His gray hair was pushed back behind his ears. There was a strange, pulsing pressure in her head, as if she were sitting at a high altitude. She looked at Atticus's hand and noticed that the ends of his fingernails were perfectly rounded. "I've been dreaming about you. I dreamt we were in a beautiful house with marble pillars and a terrace stretching out over the sea."

"I had a dream about you," Ada said. "I dreamt I had your body." He closed his eyes. A group of women in colorful outfits approached the café, and neither of them spoke until the street had emptied again, the women tucked away inside.

"Tell me something about yourself," Atticus said.

"There isn't anything to tell." She wanted to reach out and put her hand over his, to feel the warmth and roughness of his tanned skin, but she didn't.

"When you stepped in front of that car," he said, "I was sure that if you died, I would die too."

Ada stood up. Her hands were still in her pockets.

"I have to go to work."

"Come to my apartment tonight," he said. His voice was urgent, but he was looking down at the pavement, as if he was afraid of what her face would show. "Please. It's number twenty-four."

Ada didn't reply. She stood beside the table for a moment, feeling like she was watching herself from the outside, trying to understand why she was leaving. Her coat was stained on the elbows with some sort of white chalk. She didn't know where it had come from. Atticus wanted her to go to his apartment. Nobody she had talked to had ever called it an apartment before. She wanted to say something but nothing came out. It felt as if a page of essential vocabulary had been ripped out of her. Atticus looked up.

"Maybe," she said. "I don't know." Everything was muted, the space around her filled with cotton wool. She felt foolish, a soldier without orders. She left a minute later, feeling Atticus's eyes trained on her as she walked away.

At the restaurant she came back to herself. The air she drew in over her tongue had a different taste. It was the first time in her life, she felt, that she could be sure of her own existence. Somebody wanted her. Remembering Atticus's sculpted fingernails, how he'd looked at the pavement after he'd invited her to his apartment, she was happy in a way that she was sure she'd never felt before. It was almost unbearable, almost painful, as if she would crumple under the pressure. She thought about kissing him, feeling his stubble against her cheek, his warm hand on the back of her neck, and found that it made her feel excited and afraid.

Her parents were the only people who had ever said they loved her. She wasn't ever sure if she believed them when they said it. When she was eight, she had overheard her mother on the phone to a friend, saying that she never understood why people thought their children were more important than anybody else.

"I love my child in the same way that I love yours," her mother said. It was late at night and Ada was crouched on the stone floor outside the kitchen. "Anything else is narcissistic."

Outside the long front window of the restaurant dining room, it began to grow dark. The restaurant was empty. Ada put a plastic candle on each table. The streetlamps came on. She remembered the number of Atticus's apartment: 24.

WHEN HER SHIFT was over, Ada walked home instead of catching the bus. It was windy and her thin hair blew across her face. She stopped in a doorway to tie it up. Her coat was too small, so whenever she lifted her arms above her head it pinched on the shoulders and dragged the sleeves almost back to the elbow. Atticus was waiting for her. She felt a surge of dread. She had only slept with one person, an erratically energetic man she met in a bar at university. Although she hadn't enjoyed it, she had enjoyed the feeling afterwards, both of their bodies covered by the same thin, gray blanket he used as a duvet. Ada had wished he would stay still, but he kept jumping up to show her things, objects from around his room. She left his house in the middle of the night, not wanting to sleep beside him, and didn't see him again.

Maybe with Atticus it would be different. Her building came into view at the end of the road. It was tall and covered in shiny plastic cladding. She found her window, on the sixth floor, and tried to count backwards to find Atticus's, but she couldn't concentrate and kept getting lost.

In the lobby she felt like she might be sick. She imagined going into Atticus's apartment and collapsing on the floor. He would carry her to the sofa and cover her in a blanket, the same heavy, geometrically patterned blanket from the photographs. There was a map of the building in the lobby, and she found apartment 24. It was on the fourth floor. She took the stairs rather than the elevator.

Outside the door she stopped. The silver 24 reflected her distorted face. Only a sliver of painted wood separated her from Atticus. She didn't know what he wanted from her. Suddenly she thought that he might be disappointed. She raised her hand to the door, imagining him waiting solemnly for her on the other side, but she didn't knock. Her hands were made of lead. She was about to turn away and go upstairs to her own apartment when Atticus opened the door.

It looked like he had just arrived from somewhere. He was wearing a dark brown suit, and when he stepped back from the door Ada saw that he still had his shoes on. They were shiny and black. She wanted to ask him where he had been, but she felt mute and stilted.

"Were you going to knock?" he asked. "I knew you were there. I was waiting."

"I don't know."

"Do you want to come in?"

Ada didn't answer immediately. Blood rushed to her face and her hands. It made her feel dizzy. Atticus looked at her, waiting silently.

"Okay," she said. He moved to the side to let her pass. The hallway was narrow but led into a large, open-plan living room, warmly lit by a standing lamp in the corner. There was framed art on the walls and a tall, well-kept plant on the floor beside the low beige sofa. One of the framed posters showed a naked man drawn in thick black lines, his erect penis partially obscured by one cupped hand. A bookshelf stood beside the curtained window, lined by neat rows of books. The door to what Ada assumed was the bedroom was closed. "It's nice," she said.

"Neil is rich." Atticus sat down at one end of the sofa. Sitting down he looked taller. Ada sat down beside him. He turned towards her and took one of her hands in his. His skin was just as she had imagined it, warm and slightly abrasive. "We don't have to do anything," he said. He shifted towards her. His eyes were bright and shiny, like the eyes of a robin in the winter. Ada looked at him and he touched her cheek. "You're beautiful."

"I'm younger than you."

"I know."

"Does it bother you?"

"I don't feel it. I feel like we're the same." He held her hand tightly, and she could feel his eagerness. "Can I hold you?"

"Yes."

He put an arm around her and she leaned in towards him. His body was broad and angular, like in the picture, but Ada felt comfortable resting against him. She put her head on his shoulder. He lightly stroked her hair.

"I feel," he said, pausing between the words, "like something is happening."

"What do you mean?"

"I feel like I'm in love with you."

"You don't know me." She felt hot and cold at the same time, as if whatever was supposed to regulate her internal stasis had failed. When he said it, she realized it was what she wanted him to say, but she didn't know why. He was a stranger, but at the same time he wasn't, at least not in the way that the people walking past on the street outside were strangers. His hand on her arm felt so familiar, as if at one point it had belonged to her instead.

"I feel like I do."

"Tell me something about myself."

"You want to be loved. Just like me."

They stayed on the couch, their heads bowed like two magnets drawn in together. Ada listened to Atticus breathing.

His body was warm. Ada felt the warmth leaching into her own skin, as if his life force was being transferred to her. She stayed very still and let it spread across her whole body, until she was wrapped tightly in a thick, heavy blanket of warmth.

After a while she felt him move.

"I have to get up early in the morning," he said. "Do you want to come to bed with me?" He said it softly, and his hair brushed Ada's cheek as he tried to look down at her.

"No," she said, sitting up. She said it too quickly. Suddenly the apartment felt claustrophobic. Although she didn't want the warm feeling to go away, the thought of sleeping beside him, and what it might involve, scared her. She didn't know if she wanted it. She felt a need to escape, to be alone in her own apartment, unobserved.

"I don't want to be apart from you," he said.

"I'll come back tomorrow."

He smiled. "Okay."

Ada stood up. She wondered if she was weak or strong for leaving. Her legs hurt from the twisted position she'd been sitting in. Atticus's hair was messy, as if he'd been asleep, but his eyes were still bright and awake. Ada could see that he was happy. As she left the apartment and closed the door softly behind her, she felt that she was happy too. The hallway was stark and cold. She went upstairs and got into bed without turning on the lights.

THE NEXT MORNING, she got an email telling her he'd gone back to California. He didn't say why. He hadn't told her he was leaving, but as she read the email, the knowledge came back to her with a jolt of recognition, as if she had known and then forgotten.

Immediately after reading it her head began to hurt, as if she was having an allergic reaction. She assumed there must have been some kind of emergency. If he had always planned to leave, surely he would have told her. It occurred to her that maybe he wanted to take her by surprise. You only start hurting people, she thought, when you want their attention. She imagined him at the airport, reading a novel on a plastic bench. She wondered if she would ever see him again. The idea that she wouldn't was unbearable.

Although her head hurt, she went for a walk in the morning sun. She didn't want to be alone in her empty apartment, which she had fled to the night before. When she passed the café where they'd sat together, she noticed that the tables had been rearranged, and where there had been two chairs, now there were four. A group, two men and two women, sat around, talking and drinking coffee. Although summer was coming, it was still cold. It was Saturday and people were out all around her. Ada wished that they would all disappear.

She wanted to find somewhere quiet. The park was full of families. Outside the Turkish grocers' tomatoes were piled in a tall pyramid. Turning a corner, she found herself on a residential street flanked by red-brick townhouses. The lowest level was below the street, and she could see into the windows of the basement apartments, which never saw the sun. Most of them had their blinds down or curtains drawn. It was like a street of closed eyes. The sun was blindingly bright and the trees were beginning to put out small green leaves. Ada sat down on a low wall. There was no reason to have assumed Atticus would stay forever. Across from her, somebody was moving out of their house and had left a display of unwanted belongings for strangers to take. Most of it was kitchenware. It had rained in the night and all the saucepans were full of water.

The pain in her head was increasing. She imagined what would have happened if she'd agreed to stay the night. They would have climbed together into the expansive bed and curled up like two small animals. Ada looked down at the pavement. She found that she couldn't imagine the rest.

On the way home she passed a shop selling men's clothes. In the window was a mannequin wearing a white shirt that looked like the one Atticus had worn the last time she'd seen him beside the pool. She went in and asked the woman behind the counter how much it was. It was expensive, but she bought it anyway, in the smallest size they carried. The woman asked her who it was for, and she said that it was a gift.

"For your boyfriend?" the woman asked.

"Yes," Ada said.

"Let me wrap it up for you," the woman said. Ada watched her take a sheet of marbled paper from a hidden drawer. It was blue and red, like the surface of Jupiter. With elegant hands, she folded it into an envelope with the shirt inside. A sticker with the shop's name was placed carefully over the opening.

Ada thanked the woman and left the shop. She was unable to believe she'd spent so much money. When she got home, she ripped apart the paper that the woman had folded so carefully. The shirt appeared in her hands. It had buttons made of something iridescent. Ada put it on in the bathroom because it was the only place in her studio with a mirror.

It was too big around her shoulders and the straight cut hugged her hips while leaving loose fabric bunched over her stomach. The white made her skin look red. She took it off. Although it had been expensive, she knew that she wouldn't return it. Folding it up, she hid it at the back of her wardrobe, where she wouldn't have to look at it again.

THAT NIGHT, FRANCESCA was having a party. It was the birthday of her friend, who Ada had never met. Before she went out, Ada replied to Atticus's email and asked him why he'd left so suddenly. She wanted him to tell her that there had been an unforeseeable catastrophe, and that he would return as soon as he was able.

On the outside Francesca's house looked like it was about to collapse. The front garden was overgrown and full of detritus. Paint was peeling off the brick and the street-facing windows had the curtains permanently drawn. Including

Francesca, five people lived there. Ada arrived early so that her cousin could help her choose something to wear. After hiding the shirt, she had been unable to dress herself and so had put back on the clothes she'd been wearing earlier. She felt vulnerable, as though her skin wasn't thick enough to hold everything in.

When she arrived, a man she didn't know answered the door. He let Ada in and asked her if she wanted anything to drink. They stood in the kitchen while they waited for Francesca.

"She went out to buy some limes," he said. Inside the house was colorful and showed none of the decay indicated by the exterior. Somebody had painted three walls of the kitchen green so that it was like standing in a forest. Large windows showed a derelict patio ringed by lights hung on thin wire. When it was dark they would be turned on.

"Do you live here?" Ada asked.

"No," the man said, "but this is my party."

"You're Patrick." He nodded. He was solid and brown-haired, with a sharp face. Ada noticed that although he couldn't be much older than her, he had wrinkles around his mouth. "Happy birthday," she said.

The front door opened and closed. Francesca came into the kitchen with a plastic bag in her hand. She opened it and took out four limes, which she put on the countertop. She didn't speak to Patrick. Ada followed her upstairs to her bedroom. The walls were the same deep red. They made Ada feel like she was looking at the inside of her own body.

"You'll like Patrick," Francesca said. "He writes plays. I told him about you."

"I wish you hadn't."

"You can just be friends," Francesca said. "Not everything is about sex." She sat down on the bed. It was neatly made. It always surprised Ada that Francesca made her bed every morning.

"Are you excited about tonight?"

"No," Francesca said. "I got fired."

Ada looked at her phone. Atticus had emailed her. He wrote that he had been imagining her swimming. He didn't answer her question. It was as if she hadn't said anything at all. She imagined herself opening the window of Francesca's bedroom and throwing herself out. She wondered if Atticus would know if she died.

Francesca had drawers full of sequined skirts and tops with feathers stitched into the sleeves, some of which she made herself on a sewing machine in the corner of her room. She got fabric scraps from a market, which she kept in a box under her bed. Often she gave things to Ada, and when they went out together they were sometimes both dressed entirely in Francesca's clothes. Going through her drawers, Ada looked for something that would make her feel like who she wanted to be, but when she tried to imagine who that was, she couldn't conjure a clear image. The problem wasn't with the clothes, she thought, but with herself. She didn't look the way she should.

"Do you have any men's shirts?" she asked.

"No," Francesca said. "You could ask Dylan."

Dylan lived in the room next to Francesca's. Through the wall they could hear him talking loudly on the phone. Ada wondered if Atticus would be jealous. The way he'd ignored her question made her feel sick. He had said that he loved her, and then he had left.

"Don't worry," she said.

When they went downstairs, the kitchen was full. Ada didn't know anyone. People were smoking cigarettes inside and all the windows were open, showing the red sky. It was like the walls were made of yawning mouths. Patrick was standing by the window that led to the patio. He was wearing a checked shirt. Ada noticed that no music was playing.

"Something's happened," he said. "Someone's died."

"Who?" Francesca asked.

"I don't know," he said. "I don't know her."

"Here?" Francesca asked. "In the house?"

"Oh," Patrick said. "No. It's Paula's friend. Olive. Nobody's seen her for a year. She just found out."

Francesca sat down in a chair that had been pulled out from the kitchen table. Ada sat down beside her. She didn't know who Paula was. There was a girl crying at the other end of the room.

"Nobody I know has ever died," Patrick said.

Francesca stood up.

"I'm going to get a drink." She squeezed around a tall boy and a curly-haired girl talking quietly to each other. Patrick turned to Ada. All around them people began to talk again. The crying girl was taken upstairs.

"Francesca told me you're a writer," he said.

"I'm not really."

"I'm a writer too. I'm writing a play about rural England." Ada looked out the window. It had started raining. Patrick was looking at her, as if he was searching for something in her face. He lit a cigarette and turned away to blow the smoke out the window. He had a soft jawline.

"Why?"

"I want to know if there's anything relevant left in thinking about landscapes."

Francesca came back before Ada could answer. She had only brought a drink for herself. Her dress was made of deep-blue sequins that sparkled under the lights. She looked so beautiful that for a moment Ada wanted to reach over and rip a handful of the sequins off and throw them at her.

"I met Olive once," Francesca said. "She showed me these awful paintings of animals bleeding to death. It was like she wanted everyone to ask her what was wrong. The strange thing was that she was one of the most beautiful people I'd ever met. She had these hands which looked like they were made of porcelain."

"That's a shame," Patrick said.

Francesca didn't reply. She sat down again and propped her head up on her hand. Ada took out her phone and checked her email. The presence of death seemed to make everybody lethargic, as if they were being dragged prematurely towards it themselves. There was another message from Atticus. She went to the shabby bathroom to look at it. Two girls were talking on the stairs. One of them had hair piled on the top of her head in a beehive shape. The stairs were narrow, and Ada had to squeeze past them to get by. They didn't seem to notice her, and didn't move to get out of the way.

"I need a new wardrobe," the girl with the beehive said, while Ada was waiting for the bathroom. "You have to take me to get one." The other girl laughed. "How much will I need to spend?"

"Not much with me," the other girl said. "I have two tops, two skirts, two pairs of jeans, and a jacket."

"Like a uniform," the beehive girl said.

The bathroom door opened and a man came out. Ada went in. The email was a picture of Atticus that he had taken in the mirror with his shirt unbuttoned to his navel. His chest was pale and broad, like a slab of damp wood. His eyes were black holes. Ada thought he looked like a doll. When she came out of the bathroom Francesca was standing nearby, talking listlessly to the curly-haired girl.

Patrick was still standing by the window. People had started to leave. Some, but not all of them, came up to him to say goodbye.

"I don't really know what to do," he said. "Did you ever know someone who died?"

"There was a man who lived with my father after he moved out," Ada said. "He died."

"I'm sorry," Patrick said.

"I never met him."

"I never met Paula's friend," Patrick said. "So I guess it doesn't matter. Nothing's changed for me."

On the wall behind Patrick's head there was a picture that someone had pinned up with thumbtacks. It showed a bowl of oranges and a blue jug on a table covered in a white cloth. The oranges were perfectly round and uniform.

AT THE END of the night, Ada got a taxi home. She hadn't had a chance to talk to Patrick alone again, but as she was leaving, he gave her his phone number.

Alone in the taxi, she took out her phone to look at Atticus's picture. The part of her that was thrilled by it had a synthetic feeling, as if she had been vacuum-sealed inside a plastic bag.

Still, the picture stared out at her. Something about it fascinated her. He was in a room with fluted sea-green walls. Behind him there was a window. Through it she could see a blue sky frothed with clouds. The edge of a wooden nightstand and the corner of a bed frame were just visible along one side. She imagined what it was like to touch the bed, feeling the hard corner beneath her fingers, leaning on it to reach something on the other side, a book lying face down on the white linen sheets.

When she got home, she opened the window and turned on the lamp beside her bed. She could hear cars driving past outside. She slept with the lamp on often. It made her feel like going to sleep was temporary, something she wasn't really supposed to do. Throughout the night she woke up almost every hour. When the light outside her window turned from black to pale blue she got up and turned the lamp off. Then for a few hours she could sleep properly.

The lamp was just below the edge of her bed, and the blanket cast a mountain range of shadows on the opposite wall. Ada imagined herself climbing up it, hand over foot. The dead girl was behind her. Her porcelain hands gripped the sharp edges of the rock. Below them was a black sea that crashed against the narrow cliffs, sending spray up so high it made their hands and faces wet.

Ada turned over so she was facing the lamp. It had a white linen cover that turned yellow when the bulb was on. She tried to imagine what Atticus was doing but found that she couldn't. She could only imagine him sitting on the loungers beside the pool. It occurred to her that she would probably never see him again. The realization made her feel placid, as if the bucket full of her anger had spilled over.

The picture appeared before her, as perfect as a painting. Atticus was looking in the mirror, his phone in his hand. Ada could see the mirror framing his reflection, but she also was the mirror, looking back at him. She closed her eyes, trying to keep the image intact. She shifted in bed, trying to get comfortable. She opened her eyes again for a moment and found that her bedroom was gone.

Atticus was in front of her. He was in a barber's chair with a black smock around his neck. A young man was cutting his hair. Atticus looked straight ahead at the mirror, straight into Ada's eyes. His tanned face was pale beneath the bright lights. Ringlets of gray hair fell away, exposing a wrinkled neck.

"How much off?" the barber asked. He was American and wore thick glasses. Ada knew that she was seeing the present moment.

"Not too much," Atticus said. "I'm nothing without it." He looked at his reflection as if examining a blurry photograph. Ada was sure he could see her, watching him from the other side.

It was like looking through the lens of a camera. When the barber was done, she saw him remove the black smock and shake the hair from it. Atticus stood up and followed him to the till to pay. He had the air of someone strained by an unfamiliar activity. He left and the door closed heavily behind him. Outside, the street was drenched in yellow sunlight. Out of the hairdressers Atticus became more confident. He walked with a kind of swinging lilt, like a pendulum. She wished that her perspective would merge with his so that she could know what it was like to be him. She had never really seen him in motion before, only walking the short distance from the poolside to the changing rooms. Looking from behind, she could almost feel where the sun met the back of his neck. He put up a hand to touch it as if sensing the same thing, brushing away the loose hair left over from the barber's cut. To his left there was a man selling plastic cups of fruit over ice. Flies buzzed around the stall. The ice melted and dripped onto the pavement. Then she was back in her bedroom listening to the cars driving past below her window.

IN THE MORNING she went to the pool. It was still dark outside when she got up, and she had a headache again. As she swam, she imagined herself as a swimming-machine: a set of rotating limbs attached to a metal box with a whirring motor inside it. She had woken up to another email from Atticus. It contained only a picture of his garden. She remembered the image of the street and the fruit stall. Atticus's reflection had been visible in the bluish tint of a shopwindow, as if his reflection was her own. She didn't wonder for a second if she had dreamt it. She knew that what she had seen was the truth.

She hadn't replied to either of his emails. It occurred to her that he might be able to look through the window that had opened between them and see her in the same way that she saw him. Just in case he could, she got changed beneath her towel even though the pool was empty. After swimming she went back upstairs and opened her computer. His garden stared out at her. It was full of foamy white flowers. A gravel path led to a house concealed somewhere out of sight amongst the foliage.

She wondered why he hadn't said he loved her again. Whatever was between them had changed. While she was looking at the picture the sun had come up outside her window.

Looking around her kitchen, she felt like she was dissolving, but had no way to stop it. He had loved her, and then he had gone away, and he had taken part of her with him. She checked her email again, but there was nothing. Unable to stay inside, she put on her coat and went down to the street, knowing it was colder than it had looked from her window. As the sun appeared at her windowsill she went to walk around the park.

The park was a diorama of muddy, gravel-studded pathways and skeletal trees. People were walking their dogs. London sometimes felt like a city overflowing with dogs. Ada sat on a bench. It was warm in the sun and cold in the shade, meaning that both were uncomfortable. She took out her phone. She had another email from Atticus. He said that she was beautiful and asked her to send him some pictures of what she did that day. Was she beautiful? What parts of her? What did it mean? Ada wondered if she was winning or losing. Not being with Atticus was like being dead. She took a picture of an emaciated tree against the blue sky, a cadaverous hand rising from a grave.

When she got home, she emailed it to him. The sun had gone behind a cloud, and she turned on the lamp again to replace the gray. Exhausted, Ada got into bed. Her sheets were white and clean. She closed her eyes.

Slowly an image came. It was semitransparent but became firmer and more saturated the longer Ada looked at it. There was a low buzz, as if her head were resting against the window of a moving car. Atticus was asleep in a large bed, illuminated by sunlight that poured through an open window. The walls of the room were the same seafoam green. On one wall hung a mirror. Because it had no frame or border, it looked like another window, reflecting the tangle of foliage in the garden and harsh blue sky visible outside the room. There was a bird calling insistently from a stone birdbath in the center of the gravel courtyard, but Atticus didn't wake up. He was so still he could have been a statue. For a moment Ada wondered if he was breathing.

She wanted to move closer to him, but she had no body. She could only shift her perspective a little in each direction, like a periscope controlled by something outside of herself. It occurred to her for the first time that she might be a tool, that someone else might be using her to watch the sleeping Atticus through her eyes. On the bedside table there was a book and a pair of glasses. On the floor was an unlabeled bottle containing some kind of ointment.

There was no way of knowing if he was real, but Ada was sure that he was. The room was so golden and sun-drenched it seemed to be a painting. Atticus was like a child when he slept, his upper lip slightly damp, and his hair matted on the pillow. Soon he would wake up and open his eyes. Was it possible that he would see her? Did it ever go both ways? Was he watching her, asleep in her bedroom in London, dreaming about him?

Ada tried to look down at herself, but she could only see the floor. It was covered partially by a faded rattan rug. Suddenly she had a feeling that she was falling. Atticus moved on the bed, shifting over to the other side. She felt herself falling into him. She could feel the softness of the bed. She stretched out with limbs that were longer than her own and opened her eyes. Instead of the sea-green wallpaper, she was looking at her own white walls. All the lights were on. She had been asleep, but she knew it wasn't a dream. Outside, the sun was high, and the sky was blue.

THE NEXT DAY she met Patrick in Covent Garden. He had asked her to meet for coffee. The impression of sleeping Atticus was still with her. Patrick was late. Ada sat under the canopy outside the café but didn't order. It was raining and the street was quiet and wet. Keeping her scarf and gloves on because of the cold, she went over the details of what she'd seen the night before. For a moment she had become Atticus. The feeling of leaving herself had opened a door inside her through which a fresh, crisp air entered, carrying with it unfamiliar sunshine. Across the street, a young woman holding a large bouquet of yellow carnations argued with her sister or her mother. Ada watched as she slammed the flowers down on the wet pavement. Instead of flying into the air, the loose petals were stuck down by the rain.

It was like she could see things from two perspectives, like she and Atticus had dug a tunnel between their separate prison cells. She wanted to know what it was like to be him all the time. The rain made a dirty river in the gutter.

Patrick arrived fifteen minutes late. He was wearing a wool scarf and a tartan coat. Ada stood up to meet him. He didn't seem aware of his lateness, or at least didn't mention it. He asked if they could sit outside so he could smoke, as long as she didn't mind the cold.

"I want to tell you about the play that I'm writing," he said. He paused. "Is it order inside or table service?"

"I think they come out to us. They might not know we're here."

"I'll go and get someone." He stood up again. While he was gone Ada checked her phone. There was nothing. After a few minutes he returned with a waiter who took their order. Instead of coffee he ordered some kind of floral tea.

"What's your play about?" Ada asked.

"People being in love," he said. "It's the only thing I think about." He paused. Ada waited for him to keep speaking. "The characters are two men stuck in a train carriage after it crashes. Nobody knows they're there. Through the window they can see a field and a lake, but they can't break the glass to get out." He paused. "That's what being in love feels like."

"It doesn't make sense," Ada said.

"Which part?"

"Surely somebody would be looking for them."

Their drinks came. Patrick's tea bag steeped in a clear pot with a flower that slowly unfurled in the hot water. He played with the string of the tea bag, folding the label into a tiny square.

"They've been forgotten about," he said. "The search and rescue mission has left them behind." He shifted around in his chair.

"I guess anything can happen in a play."

"Maybe one of the men is injured," Patrick said. "So the other one can't leave him to look for help."

"Which one is you?"

"I don't know. When I was an actor, I always wanted to play a character who was dying of an injury. I thought it would make me look vulnerable."

"Have you ever been injured?"

"No," he said. "Have you?"

"I broke my wrist once."

"I worry that not enough bad things have happened to me," he said. Ada looked at him. The wrinkles around his mouth disappeared when he spoke. He rolled a cigarette and lit it with a small red lighter.

"Some people make things up," Ada said. "You could do that."

"I can't even imagine what I'd make up. I think I'd like it if I could say that my father hit me. Or even if he wanted me to stay on the farm instead of moving to London."

"Did he?"

"No. He's always been very supportive." Patrick sat back in his chair. Behind him the sky was low and gray. They were the only people sitting outside. Inside, the coffee shop was full and the windows were fogged up with condensation. "What're you writing at the moment?" he asked.

"I'm writing a novel about my parents' divorce."

"I thought you wrote science fiction."

"I wrote some science-fiction short stories. Nobody ever liked them. Now I'm trying something different."

"Why did your parents get divorced?"

"My father wanted to become a bodybuilder." She looked at the coffee in her cup, which had gone cold. The froth had collapsed into a flat brown lake. She emptied a packet of sugar into it and stirred it around. It stayed stubbornly in granular form. "You should make up something less obvious," she said. "So people believe it."

"I don't think I really need to make anything up," he said. "It's just impossible to know what the bad things really are."

When they left the coffee shop Patrick walked a short way with her. The rain had turned to mist, which collected on her gloves and scarf. At the bus stop she waved goodbye as he disappeared up the empty street. She realized too late that she hadn't asked him where he lived. She had no idea how long it had taken him to get to the café, or where he was going.

On the way back she pretended that she was Atticus. When she caught sight of her reflection in the bus window, she was upset to see that her appearance was still her own and avoided looking at it again.

WHEN SHE GOT home Atticus had emailed her again. Ada wondered how somebody could send so many messages without receiving any in return. It was like she didn't need to exist. He was talking to himself through her. He said he wanted her to read his novel. It was written in the first person from a woman's perspective. He said that he'd always felt closer to women than men, and that the woman was really supposed to be him.

Finally, there was something he wanted her to do. She emailed back and said that she would read it. He replied immediately. The manuscript was attached.

Ada read the whole thing in one sitting. It was written as if it were a woman's diary. She was extremely religious, but at the end of the story she attacked her cold husband, who ignored her, and killed him in their kitchen with a cast-iron pan. Then she immediately turned herself in to the police, tormented with guilt. Ada couldn't understand how the woman was Atticus.

The only section that stood out to her was the description of the woman's childhood home. The house Atticus was describing was the one Ada had grown up in. The similarities were vague, but Ada recognized them: the uncarpeted wooden stairs, the heavy, dusty curtains that covered the windows in the winter, the back windows that looked out towards the sea, even the bats that periodically made a home in their attic and had to be removed under the cover of night. Ada remembered her mother balancing precariously at the top of a ladder, spraying expandable foam into the tiny hole through which they'd seen the bats emerge at sunset. In the morning they had nowhere to return to, and so they tucked themselves away anywhere they could find. There was a ceramic sundial above the front door, and when Ada passed beneath it, she looked up to see an impossible number of bats lined up in the narrow space behind it.

At the end of the novel, the woman returned to the house. In the bedroom, hidden beneath a corner of the carpet, she found a small doll she had hidden as a child. Ada remembered hiding a plastic doll in the same way before her mother had sold the house when she went to university. Although she couldn't remember having thought about it before, Ada could remember the beige color of the carpet that she'd pried up with her fingernails. The doll had been smaller than her thumb.

They were connected. Atticus had her memories. The woman in his novel was both of them. When Ada went to sleep, she dreamt that she was screaming at him from too far away a distance to be heard.

THE NEXT MORNING things seemed clearer. The sky was brilliantly blue and the small clouds moved quickly. It wasn't possible that Atticus knew about the doll. The house that Ada had lived in was two hours outside of London. There was no way that Atticus could have described it with so much accuracy. She must have made it up, filling in his description with her own imagination.

Her mother had sold the house to a musician who wanted a quiet place close to Norwich. Ada was sure that she would let her in to look around. She was sure that the house wouldn't be how she remembered it, how Atticus had written it. It was like he had overwritten her memory. There was a train every hour that would take her to Norwich, and from there, a bus. She had done the journey countless times before, going into London with her mother.

She had to wait at the station. Pigeons fluttered around beneath the domed ceiling. She thought about telling her mother she was going to visit their old house but decided not to.

On the train, watching the flat fields go by, she thought about her father. When Ada was ten, he had gone on a strict diet. He had become interested in bodybuilding. Every day he went to the gym after work. He ate his meals apart from Ada and her mother, cooking in huge quantities once a week on a Sunday night. Two shelves in the fridge were reserved for his slim black Tupperware. He bought a blow-up mattress so that he could sleep on the floor in the basement, surrounded by equipment that he'd bought online. He stopped coming upstairs except to eat or use the bathroom. Sometimes in the middle of the night Ada would hear him creep up to the living room to watch TV. Eventually he moved out of the house and her mother divorced him. Ada talked to him on the phone once a month.

After he left, her mother began to lose weight. She lost so much that Ada was sometimes unable to recognize her. She would starve herself for days before entering a frenzy of hunger and eating everything in the house. Then she would go to bed in her big, dark room at the top of the house and sleep until Ada woke her up. Her mother sometimes told people that Ada's father denied her existence. It was better than the reality, which was that he was indifferent to her. It seemed to Ada that there was nothing wrong with adjusting the facts if it made things simpler and easier to understand. After a while, Ada began to wonder if her mother would ever move on. The lies she told replaced the truth, which meant that she always had a reason to be angry. At least her father, in leaving, had shown that he didn't care either way, which seemed to Ada a show of ultimate strength. When they spoke on the phone, he was always cheerful.

She arrived in Norwich. It was a bright day that made Ada's mouth dry. The buildings were mostly red brick, and when the sun shone, they all seemed to glow, so that the whole town felt like a sunset. The bus stop was just outside the station. Litter covered the ground. While Ada waited, she thought about Atticus, what it would be like to be close to him. She imagined them twisted up together like two pieces of wire, tight enough to erase any distance between them.

The bus came and she got on it. She was the only passenger. It took her out of Norwich and into the marshy countryside that bordered the North Sea. It was known for its flatness and lack of character, and as Ada watched it pass outside her window, she felt an affinity with it. She had loved the feeling of the salt-heavy clay beneath her bare feet, and the long-necked birds that made their homes in the shallow rivers that broke the coastline into a series of low-slung promontories.

The house came into view. It stood right up against the road, and in the summer Ada had been able to look out her window and see straight into the motor homes that passed through the village on their way to the campsite. She got off the bus and walked the short distance to the door. It didn't look like anybody was in, but she knocked anyway. After a long wait a woman answered the door.

"I used to live here," Ada said. "I was wondering if I could look around."

Several moments passed before she answered. She looked at Ada with what Ada could only assume was anger. She had red hair that lay flat against her head and very pale, freckled skin. Tattoos encased her shoulders like two big hands.

"I bought the house off Lydia Richman," she said, finally.

"I'm Ada Richman," Ada said. "She's my mother. I grew up here."

"She said she had a daughter," the woman said. "You're not going to steal anything?"

"No," Ada said. The woman opened the door wider, so that Ada could pass through.

"I'm doing some work in the garden," she said. "Let me know when you're done and I'll see you back out." She disappeared down the dark hallway.

Ada stood in front of the staircase. To her relief, it was carpeted, although the carpet looked new. It had been several years since they'd moved out. The woman could have changed any number of things. She went into the living room. The walls were painted a bright hyacinth blue rather than the white Ada remembered. In one corner stood a keyboard.

Heavy curtains hung around the windows, pulled back to let the light in, but they were linen rather than velvet, patterned with gold fleurs-de-lis.

It was different. Ada could hear the sound of the woman digging in the sun-soaked garden. When she had lived there, the garden had been a square of mud tangled with briars. Hoping that the woman wouldn't come back inside, she went up the stairs to where her bedroom had been. As in the living room, the color of the walls had changed, but the carpet was the same. Ada could see the spot where she'd spilled coffee beside her bed. Now the bed was on the other side of the room. Looking at it, Ada realized it was a different bed entirely.

She went to the corner where she remembered hiding the doll. The carpet was tacked down, but she pulled the edge up and it came away from the floor. At first, she thought there was nothing there, but she pulled at it a little more, and there it was, a tiny plastic figurine of a shepherdess with a miniature crook.

Ada pushed the carpet back down. The room seemed suddenly too bright. She went back down the stairs and called out to the woman in the garden that she was leaving. The woman didn't look up from the flower bed where she was planting something. Her trousers were caked in mud. Ada went out into the street and closed the door behind her. Suddenly she regretted not taking the doll as some kind of proof, but there was no way to go back. Why hadn't she taken it? Maybe she hadn't even really seen it there. Now that it wasn't right in front of her, she couldn't be sure that she hadn't made it up.

THE JOURNEY HOME passed in a series of stationary images. When Ada got back to her apartment, it was raining. It seemed strange that it could be so sunny in Norwich but rain in London. She wanted to ask Atticus about the house and the doll but was afraid he would pretend not to know what she was talking about. It was possible he didn't know that the house and the memories he was describing were hers, that he thought he'd just made it up. She decided not to reply until she knew exactly what she wanted to say.

She felt the roof of her mouth with her tongue. The lump was there. She went into the bathroom to look at it in the mirror. If she tilted her head back into the light, she could just about see it. It was long, stretching nearly from the back of her front teeth to the end of her soft palate. She reached a finger into her mouth and felt it. It was hard, more like bone than cartilage or tissue. She pressed her fingernail into it. It left a crescent-shaped indentation that she could feel with her tongue. She took a pair of tweezers from the bathroom cabinet and pinched them around it. It had no feeling. She pulled at it gently.

There was a brilliant white light, and for a moment she was completely blind, as if she had been in a dark room and somebody had thrown back the curtains. There was no pain, but she felt a deep physical discomfort, as if she had been made aware of a tumor growing inside her. She could see Atticus. He was sitting at a wooden desk in some kind of study. From the watery light she knew it was very early in the morning. She could hear birdsong coming in through the window. Telephone wires turned what she could see of the sky outside into a grid. He had his computer open. She wanted to see what was on the screen, but she was too far away. She looked around. The room was small, empty apart from the desk and a cabinet in the corner. It had a carpet made of some kind of woven reed or grass. She noticed that Atticus had his shoes on, as if he was about to leave for somewhere. There were two framed photographs on the wall above the desk. Both of them were black and white. One was of a naked woman. Her face was turned away from the camera. She had long hair. The other showed two small children playing in a garden. Ada knew looking at them that they were Atticus's wife and children.

Ada felt sick. She was in her bathroom again and the lump had begun to ache. Putting the tweezers down beside the sink, she knew she had seen inside Atticus's head. She went back into the kitchen. Flurries of small, bright stars rushed around in front of her eyes. His email was still open on her computer. In anger she deleted it. Maybe it would sever the connection, she thought, like cutting a phone line. For the first time she felt afraid of what was happening. Her body and her life weren't completely her own. Even her thoughts felt strange and wrong. All she could think about was Atticus. She felt that she was becoming two people, her vision bisecting into two translucent images laid across each other, like two photographic negatives.

She could still see his study as clearly as her own kitchen, with the photograph of the naked woman above the desk. Of course he was married. Ada stood up abruptly and went into the bedroom, as if she could shake off the thought, or somehow evade it. She wondered if she might be insane. She looked up at the ceiling. Someone tell me what's going on, she thought. What am I supposed to do? She opened her wardrobe and stared at the clothes inside. Who was she? She could feel the rough grass matting of Atticus's study beneath her feet, and although her room was entirely in the shade, she could feel the warmth of a hot sun on her arm.

THE NEXT AFTERNOON Francesca called. Ada woke up to the ringing of the phone and realized she'd been asleep since the previous evening. It was the longest she'd ever slept. She hadn't dreamt at all.

"I've got an emergency," Francesca said. "I need you to come with me to the hospital."

Ada put her coat on and called a taxi to Francesca's apartment. Francesca was waiting on the street, wrapped in a thick coat, although it was warm outside. She was pale. She got into the taxi. Ada leaned forwards.

"We need to go to the hospital," she said to the driver. He glanced backwards at Francesca. Ada thought he was going to ask what was wrong with her.

"Which one?" he said.

"I don't know. The closest one." Reluctantly he turned back around. Ada noticed that his head was covered in sweat. It soaked into the neck of his polo shirt. She got the sense that he wanted to refuse them. She turned to face Francesca. She was leaning against the window, eyes closed. There was a flushed, red spot on her cheek.

"What happened?"

"I'm not sure." It took her a moment to answer. She was breathing heavily. "I woke up this morning and my stomach hurt. Then half an hour ago I started bleeding."

There was traffic. Ada stared out the window. The car stopped and started. She didn't ask Francesca if the bleeding was ongoing. She could tell that the cabdriver was listening to them. When they got to the hospital, she helped Francesca through the glass doors of the emergency room. It was quiet. A woman in blue scrubs, a doctor or a nurse, approached them. She had her hair in a bun and wore a lot of makeup, so much that her face shone wetly beneath the bright lights, as if she was wearing a damp, skin-colored mask with dark holes around her bright, attentive eyes.

"What's happened here?" The doctor took Francesca by the elbow and helped her to a chair.

"I think I'm having a miscarriage," Francesca said.

"Are you pregnant?"

"I don't know." She sighed and closed her eyes.

"Let's get you to an examination room." The doctor helped Francesca stand up again. Ada noticed a small spot of blood on the chair. She watched Francesca make her way slowly across the wide linoleum floor and disappear behind a screen.

She looked around. She would have to call the restaurant and cancel her shift. Her manager was understanding in cases of emergency. The emergency room was large and cluttered. Medical equipment stood patiently between rows of plastic chairs and vending machines. In the middle was a reception desk, behind which a young woman talked on the phone in a low, calm voice. On the walls were informational posters detailing the symptoms of viral meningitis and chlamydia.

She looked around at the other people waiting. A third of the plastic chairs were occupied. A young man sat across from her, reading a book. To her left were two old women, one with a large purple bruise on her elbow. She was holding her arm straight out in front of her. Doctors and nurses in blue-and-white uniforms moved around the space quietly and fluidly, like chess pieces. There was a vending machine beside her. She bought a chocolate bar and put it in her bag. At a different vending machine, she bought a bottle of water. When she sat back down, the boy with the book smiled at her. She smiled back. She felt the presence of bodies all around her. She didn't like to think of herself as a body. People became bodies when there was something wrong with them. The doctors and nurses, however, had an ethereal quality, as if by recognizing the existence of other people's bodies, by attending to them, they had gotten rid of their own. She wondered if it was true that doctors never fell ill.

She went to the bathroom. It was empty. She opened her mouth and looked at the lump in the long mirror. It was the same. It occurred to her that she could show it to a doctor. What would happen if they tried to remove it? She went back out to the waiting room. Francesca was still behind the screen. While Ada was gone, somebody had cleaned up the spot of blood on the chair.

Ada sat back down. She wondered if Francesca really had been pregnant, or if it was something else. She felt as if she were watching her act out some kind of ritualistic performance rather than suffering something real. On the wall across from Ada was a flyer that caught her attention, and she leaned forwards to read it. In the middle of the fine print was this line: "Atticus is thinking about you."

He was thinking about her. She knew that he was. As soon as she'd read it the doctor came out from behind the screen and crossed the room towards her. Ada stood up.

"Francesca's just gone to talk to the counselor," the doctor said. Ada thanked her, and the doctor walked away. Ada sat back down. She had expected the doctor to tell her that everything was okay. Instead, she would have to wait longer. She felt tired and wanted to go home. She wondered what Atticus was doing. She imagined him in his office and remembered the feeling of the warm sun on her arm. He was waiting for her response to his book. He might email her again, but she knew she would ignore him. Suddenly she felt lonely. She had appreciated his questions. Not many people asked her questions.

Eventually Francesca came out. Her face had more color.

"My dad's driving down. He'll be here at midnight," she said.

"I'll come back to yours," Ada said. She waited for her cousin to say that nothing was wrong, but Francesca remained silent. Ada led her through the double glass doors. In the taxi, Francesca fell asleep. She woke up when they arrived at her house. Ada made her bed while she disappeared into the bathroom for a long time. When she came out, her hair was wet, and she got into bed without bothering to dry it. Outside it was getting dark. Ada closed her curtains and turned on the lamp, then went to sit in the living room. None of the friends Francesca lived with were home. Ada wondered where they all were. Their absence made the house dark and lonely. She sat upright, anxious that somebody might come in.

Two hours later Francesca appeared. Her hair was still damp. She came to sit beside Ada on the sofa, pulling a scratchy tartan blanket over her legs.

"Dad will be here soon," she said.

"I'll go home," Ada said. They sat together in silence for a minute. "What did the doctor say?"

"I might be anemic. They gave me some iron tablets." Ada was reluctant to press her. She felt as if everything was happening very far away.

"What was it that happened?" Ada asked.

"It was nothing." Francesca stared at the wall. "I just got my period. The doctor said there was nothing wrong. I said I wanted to talk to the counselor anyway. She said she couldn't see what I was so upset about."

"Why were you upset?" Francesca's face seemed to droop downwards like a melting candle.

"I just felt like something was wrong." She stopped. On the wall opposite Ada was a painting of two dancing woman set against a background of colorful shapes. Francesca looked down at the sofa and rubbed her finger along the raised seam at the edge of the cushion cover. "I thought if it was a miscarriage or something at least people would take me seriously. You don't have to explain anything. And it's someone's fault because someone had to get you pregnant, so you have someone to be angry at."

"Why do you need someone to be angry at?"

"I don't know. Everything just feels unfair. I want it not to be all my fault."

Ada looked at the painting. The two dancing women had been abstracted to a pair of round, faceless shapes. She wanted to ask who had painted it.

The doorbell rang. Ada saw that Francesca was crying. She had trouble processing it, as if she had forgotten what crying meant.

"Don't tell Dad," Francesca said. "I told him it was a miscarriage. I don't want him to think I'm a liar."

"I won't." Ada stood up.

"Will you look in the cupboard?"

Ada went over to the wardrobe and opened it. She knew Francesca wouldn't calm down unless she moved all the clothes out of the way and looked behind them. After the cupboard, she raised the blind and opened the window so that she could look out. When she closed it and turned back around, Francesca had stopped crying.

"There's nobody there," she said.

"I'm weak," her cousin said. "That's my problem. On the inside and outside. I can't be a good person, because I'm too weak to make the right decisions."

On her way down Ada passed her uncle—her mother's brother—on the stairs.

"Thanks so much for looking after her," he said.

"It was nothing," she said.

She got home at midnight. Wanting somebody to talk to, she thought about writing to Atticus and telling him what had happened. She had a feeling that things were spinning out of control. Too tired to turn on the lights, again she sat in the dark. She worried she had let Francesca down. Ada had been willing to pretend with her. Outside the window, the dense clouds were tinted orange by pollution.

There was something like a star showing through the clouds, a small point of red light that sat just above the uppermost line of the tallest building in view. At first, she thought it was a plane taking off from City Airport, but after watching for a while she realized it was static, like somebody shining a torch at her from very far away. She turned away from the window and suddenly became aware of a red circle cast onto the back wall of her kitchen. It was large and perfectly round. It filled the room with a red glow. She stood without moving for a moment, then went over to the wall and turned on the light. The red circle disappeared.

ADA WOKE UP late again the next morning. Her room was filled with pale daylight. She'd dreamt that she was in Atticus's garden, but he wasn't there. A brightly colored bird dipped itself in the birdbath. A wooden house, painted white with dark beams around the doors and windows, stood before her. Purple and white irises nodded and swung in the breeze.

There was a child on the path, a girl in a blue dress. Ada called to the girl but she didn't seem to hear. She was digging a hole in the gravel, and the dust was covering her from head to toe. Ada watched as Atticus's narrow silhouette appeared at the door. He seemed taller, in a tan suit and shoes with a slight heel that shone in the evening light.

"Ada," he called. In the dream Ada was filled with joy until she tried to move forwards and realized she couldn't. The girl turned around. Atticus was coming down the path towards her. "Ada," he said again. "What are you doing?"

When he reached the child, he picked her up. With a small, trusting hand she held on to his shoulder. The dust that had covered her transferred itself to Atticus's suit. They went back up the path and into the cool shadow of the house, leaving Ada alone in the garden.

When she woke up, it was after midday. She thought vaguely that she should go swimming, but she felt heavy and tired. She didn't want to go down to the pool. She could barely remember why she had ever gone in the first place. She wondered if Atticus missed her. He had been too confident. Genuine interest doesn't feel like that, she thought. It should feel a little like being ignored.

She decided that she would stay in bed all day. There was a small brown stain on her wall, and she stared at it. Her body felt like it was made of sand. She imagined somebody picking up a handful of it and crumbling it between their fingers. Atticus would be waiting to hear what she thought about his book. Part of her wished desperately for him to come back to London, but then she remembered the picture of the naked woman and the rattan carpeting of his office. She thought about telling everything to Patrick, but she was scared of him discovering what her life was really like.

As she dressed, she looked around at her room. The white walls were bare. The only color came from the yellow blanket on the bed. On the windowsill sat two desultory plants that her mother had bought her when she'd moved in. She didn't like to take care of things. There was a small bookshelf and a wooden table. She felt as if she were seeing it all for the first time. She tried to remember something from her childhood, any minor detail, but nothing came to mind. Where is Atticus? she thought. What is he doing? What is he thinking about?

She picked up a book from her bedside table. She tried to read it, but the words kept rearranging themselves. If she stopped concentrating it became Atticus's novel. She put it down and went into the bathroom. It was dark. She turned on the light. When she looked in the mirror, it was Atticus's face that she saw reflected back at her.

She moved her hand. Atticus's hand moved in response. Reaching up to touch her face, she saw Atticus's fingers meet his stubbled cheek. In the harsh light of her bathroom, he looked like a bird of prey, with his hooked nose and sallow cheeks. Ada slowly returned her hand to her side. She didn't dare move quickly in case the vision disappeared. In the mirror Atticus wore a white shirt. Without looking down, Ada knew that it was different from the one she was wearing. It wasn't a reflection. It was Atticus, looking at her from the other side of the glass.

She nodded her head, and Atticus nodded back. He must be in the bathroom of his house, she thought, looking in the mirror and seeing me reflected back to him. Stretching out her hand she touched the glass, and felt the warmth of Atticus's finger on the other side. It occurred to her that it might be Atticus leading their movements. She unbuttoned her shirt at the neck. A triangle of tanned skin appeared at Atticus's throat. She unbuttoned it the rest of the way and took it off. Then she took off her trousers, and her underwear, until she was standing naked in front of the mirror. Atticus looked back at her, his body flooded in the light of the bathroom.

LATER SHE MET Patrick at a bar. He was late again, and Ada sat outside to wait for him. Absentmindedly she touched her face. She half expected to feel the roughness of Atticus's stubble beneath her fingers. It was late, and inside the bar was full, but nobody else sat at the long wooden tables set up on the street. Each one was lit up by an electric heater. Ada could feel the warmth on the back of her neck, and when she looked at her hands it was like they were glowing from the inside. Walking from the bus stop, she had jumped back from a parked car, convinced that it had started to roll towards her.

Patrick was later than he had been the last time. Ada wondered if she should buy a drink, but she didn't want him to think that she noticed his lateness, or that she had arrived so much earlier than him. She sat totally still as the time passed, like a statue, looking down at the stained tabletop. All she could think about was Atticus. She wondered what Patrick would say if she told him about what was happening to her. There was a chance that he would accept it, but he wouldn't really believe her. It seemed possible to Ada that Atticus had never even been real, or that maybe it was Ada who was imaginary. She had never told anyone about hiding the toy. Maybe he thought Ada's memories were his own. She checked her phone. There was nothing from Patrick. It occurred to her that he might not come. She felt like she and Atticus were the only people in the universe.

When Patrick arrived, she stood up to hug him. His face was wet from rain. Ada hadn't realized it was raining. When she looked up, she saw that she had been sitting under a corrugated plastic roof.

He disappeared again, and it was a while until she realized he had gone to get them drinks. When he came back, it felt like hours had passed. He sat down opposite her.

"How are you?" she asked. She had to concentrate to know what to say. She worried that everything was leaking out of her, that she would be left to communicate with a series of animal noises, because she had forgotten how to formulate words.

"I finished the first draft of my play. I've been sending it around to agents."

"Have any got back to you?"

"No." He paused to take a long sip of his beer. "I've been taking a lot of walks in the countryside."

"That sounds nice."

He shifted slightly on the bench. Ada felt sick, like she was trying to look at two things at once. To stabilize herself, she focused on a point in the dark street. The rain had stopped. It was like her thoughts belonged to somebody else, as if Atticus was inside her head, taking her over.

"I'm sorry," she said. "I don't feel very well."

"Do you need to go home?"

"Maybe." Ada was embarrassed. "I'm sorry," she said again.

"Don't worry. I think there's something going around." He stood up. "I'll walk you to the bus stop."

They went out into the street. He put his heavy, solid arm around her. It was like being pressed against a concrete wall, as if he weren't a person, but a structure. She noticed he smelled of sweat.

"Something bad is happening to me," she said. "But I don't know how to explain it." He looked at her. They sat down on the bench at the bus stop.

"I'll wait with you," he said. "Tell me what's wrong."

"It's like I'm dissolving," she said. "When I look at things it's like I'm looking at them from all different directions. All my thoughts keep sliding around because there's nothing to hold them down. It's like trying to fill a sieve up with dust."

Patrick sat with his legs crossed and his hands in his pockets. In the gap between his coat and his trousers his wrists were very white. He leaned slightly towards her, so their shoulders were touching. Small white lights danced around in front of her eyes. She hoped the bus would come.

"You're lonely," he said. Ada felt as if he had put his hand around her and squeezed until everything inside had been crushed into a red pulp. She wasn't lonely—she had Atticus. It was impossible to be lonely if you were more than one person. It was something else, something that she didn't understand. The bus came, and she found a seat beside a window. Patrick waved to her as it pulled away, and it seemed to her that at the last second his face changed and became that of someone she didn't recognize. The minute the bus turned the corner, and he could no longer see her, she started to cry.

ADA WOKE UP in a white room that she had never seen before. She didn't remember going home or going to bed. The first thing she noticed was that the light wasn't coming from a single point, but from everywhere.

She was lying on a sofa. In front of it there was a table with a chair tucked under it. The room was perfectly square. On one side was a door. As she looked at it, she imagined who might come through it. The person she pictured was a man with smooth skin and blue eyes, dressed in a doctor's coat. A moment after she'd thought of him, the door opened and he came in.

She expected him to pull out the chair and sit at the table, but instead he sat next to her on the sofa, leaving enough room that they could comfortably face each other. He had the blue eyes that she'd thought of. His skin was almost completely devoid of marks or texture. His hair was very thin and soft, like baby's hair.

"Don't be scared," he said.

"I'm not," Ada said. "I was just thinking about you." Like she'd imagined, he was wearing a doctor's coat and had a stethoscope hanging around his neck. "Are you a doctor?" she asked.

"No," he said.

"Who are you?"

"I've been feeding you information." Ada nodded. It made sense. "It's nice to meet you," he said.

"Why am I here?"

"We think we can help you." He paused. She stayed silent to indicate that he should go on. "We want to replace your body with an identical synthetic copy."

"Why would you do that?" She looked around the room. There was nothing on the walls, and no furniture apart from the table and the sofa. Despite the lack of detail, she felt strangely uncurious.

"We think it's the solution to the problems you've been having. We've been monitoring you."

"Why?"

"It was random, part of a study. We gave you the implant in your mouth when you were a child. We want to help you."

"You've been watching me for my whole life."

"We wanted to know what would happen if we gave you access to the truth."

"What did happen?"

For a minute the man was silent. Ada wondered what they'd done wrong. She felt strangely happy, as if she'd been given a piece of good news. Someone cares about me, she thought, enough to watch my every move.

The man continued speaking.

"It's not knowledge that helps. That's why we're moving on to the next stage. We hope that a synthetic body will help you become more autonomous."

"I am autonomous," Ada said. Maybe they knew something she didn't. She tried to picture herself but found she couldn't remember what she looked like.

"Please," the man said, "let us try. We're sorry things have been difficult so far."

"Okay." She was surprised by how easily acceptance came.

"I think you're making the right choice. This could turn out to be a very good thing." He stood up. As he stood Ada noticed that the skin on his hands was smooth and unlined, even where the fingers bent. He left through the same door. Something about him reminded her of her father. The room was warm. She lay back down on the sofa and closed her eyes. Just as she drifted off, she realized she had forgotten to ask about Atticus, but she supposed that they already knew.

Part 2

Her bedroom was cold. She had left the window open before going out to meet Patrick. The blue light told her it was early in the morning. She got out of bed and went into the bathroom. She looked at herself in the mirror. Nothing had changed. She opened her mouth. The lump was gone. There was no trace of it, no scarring or void where it had been removed.

In the swimming pool Ada swam lengths slowly and rhythmically. Her body felt the same, but her mind was empty. She held on to a sense of quietness, stillness. When she was done, she went back upstairs and got dressed. She looked in the mirror and pinched the skin on her arm. It went white, then red. Everything was exactly the same. She opened her laptop and saw she had an email from Atticus. It said that he loved her and that he didn't want to be without her. "I dream about you every night," he wrote, "as if I'm falling into you, becoming you." He had left because of his wife, who had fallen down the stairs and broken her leg, but he would leave her now to be with Ada. Reading it made her feel nothing. The connection between them had been severed.

She looked at her phone. Her father was calling her.

"How are you?" he asked when she picked up. It sounded like he was driving. He always called her from the car. The speaker turned his voice into a mechanical echo. Often Ada cried after they talked without knowing why.

"I'm fine," she said. "I just went swimming."

"You're always swimming," he said. "I don't know why you don't come to the gym with me."

"I don't want to come to the gym," Ada said. "I don't like how it makes you look."

"There's nothing wrong with being strong," her father said. There was silence. "I had a dream about you last night," he said. "I wanted to tell you about it."

"Okay," Ada said.

"I was at a party, and it was full of everyone I knew when I was your age, but you were there as well. It was in the house my sister rented in Leeds. At the end of the night everybody started going home, and as I was saying goodbye to everybody, I realized I had nowhere to go. Finally, I said goodbye to you. You were going off somewhere without me, but I didn't know where."

Ada wondered if he somehow knew what had happened. Sometimes she suspected he made up his dreams to make her feel sorry for him. It was the only way he could talk about how he felt. She remembered a dream she'd had shortly after he'd moved out. He'd been a giant, walking down the lane outside their house, so tall that he'd walked over her without seeing her. She wanted to tell him about the body replacement, but he, despite his dream, would understand the least of anyone she knew.

"Where're you going now?" she asked.

"Home," he said. "I've been in Canterbury." He lived in London, on the other side of the river from Ada, in a small house with a long, narrow garden. As far as Ada knew, he hadn't had a relationship since leaving her mother. "Are you writing anything?" he asked.

"Not at the moment," she said. Everyone was always asking her what she was writing, as if her life had a gap that needed filling in.

"I'm sorry to hear that." Ada knew already that he wouldn't ask what was wrong, just like she didn't ask why he'd gone to Canterbury. He lived inside himself as if he were in a private secret garden, where everything within was more appealing than whatever was on the outside. "I've got to go," he said. "I'm nearly home."

Ada hung up. She put the phone down and looked at her hand, resting on the table. The skin was dry. There was a small scar on her thumb from an accident she'd had as a child, trying to carve a giraffe out of wood. She pictured her father's face. He was very pale, paler than her, with thin red hair and blue eyes. His family was German. Ada tried to remember what it had been like to live with him. Her childhood felt blurry and far away. She knew that the years had been filled with something—going to school, going on holiday, but she couldn't remember the specifics, where they'd been, or what her school uniform looked like. Her mother had boxes of photographs that showed a family. It occurred to Ada that they no longer belonged to her. Her body had been manufactured. It came from no one. She wondered what it was made of. Her skin felt the same. Her shoulders ached from swimming. What would it look like if she were cut open? Had they replicated all her organs? Would it just be flesh-colored foam, like the stuffing of a cushion?

She sat at her desk. She knew she should work, but she didn't want to. Instead, she reread Atticus's email. The man in the white room had said the new body would fix whatever had gone wrong. There would be no more visions. Atticus was just another person, no more or less significant than anybody else. He couldn't love her because he didn't know her. It wasn't real. She felt a rush of exhilaration.

Getting up from her desk, she went into the kitchen and took a small, sharp knife from the top drawer. She pressed it against the end of her middle finger. A bead of watery red blood sprung up beneath it. For some reason she had expected it to be a different color or texture. She put the knife back in the drawer.

The man hadn't given her much information. She wondered if she would age like other people, if she still needed to eat and sleep, or if the body sustained itself. After swimming, she was hungry. If anything had changed on the outside they would have told her. It was the inside that was different: although she was alone, she didn't feel so. It was like the empty space inside her had been filled up with concrete.

THAT EVENING SHE went to see a film with Patrick. She met him outside the cinema. He walked down the street wheeling his bicycle beside him. She didn't know anything about the film he wanted to see. He was waiting on the street when she arrived. She looked at her phone and realized that she was five minutes late.

"I bought you a ticket," he said. They went inside. The cinema was in an old building that had been restored. There was only one screen, bordered by a red velvet curtain that fell all the way from the ceiling, as if they were seated at a theater. They found their seats at the back. The chairs were rigid and new. "I don't know why we knock down old buildings instead of restoring them," Patrick said. "Only old buildings have character."

"I live in a newbuild," Ada said.

"I don't know how you do it. They don't have any identity. I like to be surrounded by things that feel authentic."

"I don't mind it," Ada said. "There's no pressure."

The film started. It was in black and white. A woman appeared on the screen and Patrick leaned over and whispered in her ear, "That's Barbara Stanwyck." Ada didn't know what he meant. She had never heard of Barbara Stanwyck. The woman had a blonde fringe that curled around in an almost perfect cylinder and severe, reptilian eyes. Ada noticed that she didn't seem to blink. With her upright posture, she was like a machine. She appeared more like an object than a person, a fluted crystal vase.

"I've never loved you, Walter," she said to the man. "Not you or anybody else." Then there was the sharp gleam of a tear in her eye, and the illusion was broken.

AFTER THE FILM was over, they got a drink. The bar was nearby, and therefore expensive. They sat outside at a narrow table. Patrick drank whiskey and smoked. He seemed relaxed. Ada drank a beer. He asked her what she'd thought of the film.

"I liked it," Ada said. It had rained while they were in the cinema. Above them the sky was gray. A window box overflowing with deep-green geraniums dripped rainwater steadily down the wall behind him. The front of the bar was covered in foliage. Terra-cotta pots trailed ivy and purple climbing flowers that Ada didn't recognize. It was like sitting in the lap of a damp, dripping forest.

"I thought you would," Patrick said. "You remind me of her."

"What do you mean?"

"She's inaccessible." Ada wondered if he was teasing her. Looking at his face, its softness offset by an acute chin, she found that it was impossible to guess what he was thinking. "It's not a bad thing," he said. Ada wondered what counted to him as authentic. The inside of the theater was brand new, newer than the building that she lived in. It just looked old on the outside. She noticed that one of his shoes was held together by duct tape.

"She's a murderer," Ada said.

"So is he," Patrick said. "That's not what it's really about." Ada watched the water running down the wall behind him. "How are you feeling?" he asked. The shame of being lonely came back to her.

"I'm a robot," she said.

"Then I suppose you don't feel anything," he said. Suddenly he seemed strangely sad. He traced the grain of the wood with one finger. There was a wet ring where his drink had sat. He spread it around so that there was a broad dark patch on the table. "Sometimes I feel like that."

"What do you mean?"

He looked at her with a sad look.

"I worry that I'm selfish," he said. "I want people to like me more than I like them. I don't feel like myself unless I have somebody to ignore." He looked at the wet table as if wondering how it had happened. While he was speaking, Ada imagined that her body began to glow. The opaque surface of her skin became translucent, and beneath it she saw a network of wires. A current hummed along her fingertips.

"You don't ignore me," Ada said.

"If I ignored you, I wouldn't see you again." He finished his drink.

"Then why do you keep trying?" Ada asked.

"I want to make things okay for you," he said. "I'm worried that you don't have anybody else. If I didn't see you, you'd disappear." Ada watched the drops running down the wall behind him and imagined reaching over his shoulder to touch them. He couldn't see it, but all he'd have to do was lean back slightly, and his shirt would be soaking wet.

A FEW DAYS later he came to use the pool. Ada didn't want him to, but when he asked, she didn't know how to refuse. She had been struggling to eat. It seemed strange to feed organic matter into a machine. She worried about something becoming clogged or caught. Her swimming costume was loose around the stomach.

Now she was afraid of getting in the water in case something malfunctioned inside her. Patrick brought a book and read stretched out beside her on a faded blue towel. His body reminded Ada of sea creatures that lived in subterranean caves and never saw the light. He was thick and pale. Blue-green veins showed in his arms.

She didn't feel attracted to him. It had surprised her when he'd undressed beside the pool and she had felt nothing. She felt that the part of her that wanted other people had been closed down. Patrick glanced up at her from his book.

"Are you going to swim?" he asked.

"I'm not sure I feel like it," she said. He had swum already. Looking at the water, she imagined short-circuiting. Patrick had brought with him a cardboard box of strawberries. Ada was aware that she hadn't eaten any, even though they were supposed to be for her. She knew that she was disappointing him.

"Paula's in the hospital," Patrick said. "It turns out she was in love with Olive."

"Who's Olive?"

"The girl who died. Paula wouldn't break up with Dylan so Olive went to Bristol. Paula thought that would be the end of it but then Olive drowned herself on the beach in front of her house."

"Oh." He looked down at his faded towel and rubbed the frayed edge between his fingers. A pressure was building inside her head. She wondered if she was being watched by the man in the doctor's coat. The pool had security cameras in all four corners of the room. She imagined a team of white-coated, smooth-skinned doctors following her every move, monitoring her progress. She longed for clear instructions.

"We could go and get a drink," Patrick said. "It's a shame to waste the afternoon."

Outside it was sunny.

"It's not wasted," Ada said. She would bore him until he left. Looking at the pool, she imagined getting into the water and watching her body come apart, her legs falling down to rest on the bottom. Patrick could dive down and catch them for her. She sat perfectly still, aware that he glanced up at her every few minutes. An old woman with stiff white hair came in and took her clothes off with arthritic slowness. She climbed into the pool and stood at the shallow end, moving her purple arms around her so that the water rippled outwards in a wide circle.

She looked at Ada, and Ada knew the man had sent her. They were watching her to make sure that she didn't get too close to Patrick. The woman started to swim in a circle, staying where it was shallow. Ada watched her. There was something artificial about her, the stiffness with which she swam, as if she wasn't accustomed to the movements of her own body.

Patrick reached out and put his hand on her ankle. Ada jerked backwards, as if she'd received an electric shock. Her elbow hit the tile floor.

"Don't touch me," she said. Abruptly she stood up. Her clothes were in a pile beside her, and she began to put them on. Patrick was apologizing, but she could only half hear him. She pulled on her trousers. The place where Patrick had touched her seemed to burn.

"Ada," he said. He began to get dressed himself. She noticed belatedly that he had a tattoo on his shoulder, a black tribal stamp that stood out like a branding mark.

The old woman looked over at them. She had seen it happen.

Ada rolled up her towel and put on her shoes. She went into the corridor, Patrick following behind her. Once the door had closed and she was out of the old woman's view, she stopped. Her hands were shaking.

"I'm sorry," she said to Patrick. Looking at him she saw that his eyes were wet.

"I'm in love with you," Patrick said. Ada stood in the middle of the hallway. She didn't know how to explain that she couldn't stand to be around him. He was so opaque. She wanted to move but found that she couldn't. Something had gone wrong with the body. The carpet was maroon with a broad pattern of interlocking beige triangles. Ada focused on a point where three triangles met one another, making a star.

"Tell me what's happening," Patrick said.

"No," she said. Able to move again, she pressed the button to call the lift.

"I don't understand," he said. He carried his towel and his book under his arm. In his hand was the box of strawberries. Animals can tell, Ada thought, when one of them has changed in some way. Birds adopted by humans and released are rejected by their species. It was the same for all woodland creatures. As a child Ada had found an injured baby rabbit, but her mother had told her to leave it, since once she picked it up, it would have the smell of her hands on it, and it could never live in the wild again.

When the lift reached the first floor, Patrick turned to her.

"Do you want me to go?" he asked.

"Yes," she said. He got out.

"I'm sorry," he said. The doors closed and the lift moved upwards.

IN THE EVENING, she went to work. After Patrick left, she'd sat on the corner of her bed watching the sun go down. Francesca came to sit at the bar. It was the first time Ada had seen her since the hospital. Every time there was a noise, she turned towards it in surprise. Ada noticed that she wasn't wearing makeup. Without it her face looked thin and pale.

When Ada asked her how she was, she said that her life was falling apart.

"What do you mean?"

"I wish I could find a way to be happy. I keep thinking I've found it but then it goes away again."

"There must be something causing it."

"There isn't. There's nothing wrong with my life. I told my therapist I think there's something wrong with me." With the tip of her finger she traced the swirling patterns in the sticky wood on top of the bar. "He said that he was inclined to agree. Happiness isn't for everyone."

"But something must have happened. Even if it was a long time ago."

"How would I know?" She stared over Ada's shoulder at the bottles stacked behind the bar. "Dad says I was a happy child, as if that should make a difference now. He just doesn't want to feel guilty." A woman sitting at a table signaled to Ada. She went over to take her order. When she came back, the chef was leaning against the doorframe, as he often did when things were quiet. Sometimes he talked to Ada about his two small twin daughters, Liza and Lina. Liza had yet to speak, even though she was seven years old. Lina interpreted for her. Ada told him what the order was. Before he went back into the kitchen he looked briefly at Francesca.

"What's his name?" Francesca said.

"Carlo."

"What's he like?"

"I don't know. I think he's married." Ada liked Carlo. In his spare time, he took pictures of butterflies. Francesca looked towards the door of the kitchen. It was slightly ajar. Her gaze lingered before she turned back to Ada.

"I saw Eric the other day, from across the street. He was with someone."

"I'm sorry," Ada said.

"It's my fault," Francesca said. "Before we broke up, I threw a glass at him. It smashed against the wall beside his head." She said it in a matter-of-fact way. Ada felt a stab of embarrassment remembering the lift doors closing in front of Patrick's face. She wanted to apologize to him but didn't know how she would explain it.

Francesca put her head down on her elbow. Her face was blank and calm.

"It's not your fault," Ada said.

"I have to take responsibility," Francesca said. "I did something wrong."

"You should forget about him," Ada said. "It doesn't matter."

"Yes," Francesca said. "It does."

The restaurant began to fill up. Ada went backwards and forwards from the kitchen to the tables. The manager was coming in later to help. Francesca stayed at the bar. She stared at the rows of bottles stacked against the wall. Every few minutes she looked at her phone. When Ada asked her if she wanted something to eat, she said she had to leave.

"I'm meeting someone," she said. "Maybe I'll come back later." She went to the bathroom to tie her hair up and splash water on her face. When she came back, Ada noticed that she had a scrap of paper in her hand. She put it in her pocket before Ada could ask her what it was.

"Do you want to do something tomorrow?" Ada said.

"Maybe," she said. "I'll call you." She put on her coat. It was green and so long it nearly touched the floor. She looked confident with it on. It seemed to make her feel better. She said goodbye and left the restaurant. Once she was out on the street, Ada watched her take the piece of paper out of her pocket. The bus stop was in front of the window. Francesca sat down to wait. Ada wondered where she was going. She imagined Francesca throwing the glass, shattering it against the wall in an explosion of kaleidoscopic rage. She and Eric had been together for two years. He had lived with her in her red room.

When she got home, she was surprised for some reason to find her apartment empty. It was as if she could feel the shape of somebody else, just around the corner, out of sight. Light from the street far below illuminated the edges of the furniture. In the dark, she sat down on the edge of her bed. She closed her eyes.

WHEN SHE OPENED them, she was in the white room. The man was sitting at the table, waiting for her. He still wore his doctor's coat. Ada hoped that he would tell her exactly what she needed to do.

"Hello," he said. She was sitting on the sofa.

"What am I doing here?"

"I wanted to check in." There was a notepad in front of him on the table. In one hand he held a pen. "Since the copy is so perfect, we were worried you might not believe us."

"Have you done this to anybody else?"

He didn't answer for a moment.

"I wouldn't want you to feel," he said, slowly, "that you were any less important."

"Why would I feel that?"

"If you weren't the only one."

"I wouldn't," Ada said. She wanted him to tell her that she was the only person that they'd ever observed. He didn't say anything.

She looked around the room. It was the same as the last time she'd been in it. The walls were made of something that seemed slightly translucent. The furniture was made of the same material.

"I love this room," she said.

"So do I," the man said.

"What's it made of?"

"I don't know. It was built by somebody else."

She looked at him. She couldn't tell his age. He was smooth and polished, as if he'd had his edges sanded away. She guessed that he also wasn't real. Maybe they had tested the bodies on themselves before giving one to her. It comforted her to feel that she still saw him as a person.

"Are you worried about me?" she asked.

"What makes you ask that?"

"You don't seem to have a reason for bringing me here."

"Do you need to know the reason?"

"Yes," Ada said. "I want to know it. I want to know about Atticus."

He smiled, but he didn't answer. There was something about him that made her relax. This time he didn't leave the room. She felt warm and tired, the same way she had last time, but she didn't want to fall asleep in front of him. Eventually she closed her eyes. Noises from the street told her that she was back in her bedroom. A man was shouting beneath her window. Looking at her phone, she saw that it was just after midnight. She turned on the light and got up off the bed. The tiredness she had felt was gone.

She got dressed and went downstairs to the street. She was frustrated that the doctor hadn't answered her question. It made her uncomfortable. There was something they didn't want her to know. It was the weekend, and the bars spilled people onto the main street. Every time she passed somebody, she imagined telling them that she wasn't real. They wouldn't believe her, but it didn't matter, because it was true. A man was standing alone on a corner, smoking a cigarette, and Ada stopped next to him while she waited for the traffic lights to change. He wore round glasses. While she waited, Ada looked at him. He looked back at her, then looked away. His trousers were ripped at the knee and he had a package wrapped in yellow paper underneath his arm. Ada guessed he was going to somebody's birthday. Eventually he looked at her again, just before the lights changed.

"You look like something scared you," he said. He crossed the street ahead of Ada in front of the waiting cars.

Ada crossed behind him. His comment didn't bother her. Everyone was scared of something. He turned the corner into a dark street and was out of her sight. The empty window of a shop showed her reflection. It was only when she looked at herself that she realized she hadn't changed her clothes in several days.

She was walking towards the restaurant. After seeing the man in the room, she felt electric and alive. Music coming out of a late-night café made the streetlamps look as if they'd been planted in rhythm. Turning onto the street where the restaurant was, she saw that the lights inside were still on. She stopped in front of it. Francesca was sitting at the bar with her back to the window. Carlo was on the other side, the cocktail shaker in his hand. He was laughing. Francesca's green coat was on the floor where it had fallen off her chair. Her bare arms were warm under the low lights. Ada turned around and walked back the way she'd come.

THE NEXT DAY was hot and sunny. Ada kept her blinds closed so that her room was dark. Listening to the faint noises outside her window, she thought about staying inside forever.

She imagined dying in her bed and rotting away before anybody came to investigate. Whoever found her would pull back the bedcover to reveal a skeleton. She wondered if the body would even decompose, or if she'd stay perfectly preserved, like a taxidermized animal.

In the middle of the morning, her mother called her. The ringtone made Ada jump. She let it ring, looking at the phone, then answered at the last possible moment.

"Are you there?" Behind her mother's voice, in the background, Ada could hear birds singing. It made her feel like she was dreaming.

"I'm here," she said.

"How are you? How is everything?"

"The same as always."

"I wanted to ask you something. I want to go on holiday somewhere hot. I want to be by the sea. We could rent a place."

"I don't know if I can."

"I'm sure you can. I can't go on my own. I think it would be good for us to spend some time together." She paused.

"I'll let you know tonight."

"I want to get on it before everything's booked."

"I don't know if I can leave work."

"A job at a restaurant is not more important than your relationship with me."

Her mother hung up the phone. Absentmindedly, Ada imagined their holiday. They would swim in the sea and lie on the beach until Ada's mother turned a dark shade of brown.

Although she tried, Ada never tanned. The main thing her mother wanted to do was talk. She wanted to know everything. Ada would walk her through the minutiae of her daily routine, and they would go over it again and again until her mother could recite it by heart, as if the things she was describing had happened to her, rather than to her daughter. There always came a point where Ada surrendered ownership of it. When she got home, she always felt curiously blank and empty, as if someone had unplugged a hole and let everything drain out.

It would be strange to see her mother with her new body. Ada felt guilty. She had done something behind her mother's back that had nullified their relationship. Although her father had tried turning his body into a machine, he couldn't get rid of the fact of their relatedness. Ada had taken the final step and cut the rope that connected them to each other. Maybe it would make her a better daughter. It would be a choice rather than an obligation. She decided that she would go on the holiday.

She got up to have a shower. In the bathroom, she looked at herself in the mirror. Her hair hung in tangled wads around her face. There were black smudges beneath her eyes where she hadn't properly removed her makeup. She looked the same as she always had, but something was slightly wrong. She looked closer. There was a mole on her shoulder that hadn't been there before. She was sure she couldn't remember ever having seen it. It was just above the crease of her armpit. She stared at it. Could they have added it in by accident? It seemed like a ridiculous mistake. They gave the impression of having been so meticulous. She got into the shower. She could ignore it. It was just a mole. She tried to rub it away, but it wouldn't go. It was like it had appeared overnight. Maybe it had always been there, and she'd just never noticed it.

Her mother would probably want to go to Greece. Some years ago she had stopped her work as a solicitor and instead worked as a consultant, which allowed her to dictate her own schedule completely. There was a house on an island that she'd found several years before and often went back to. It had no electricity and only intermittent running water, but it was walking distance from the sea. Sometimes she went for as long as a month. She seemed to be happy only when she was on holiday. If she was at home, she was always thinking of somewhere apart from where she was and planning how to get there.

Ada got out of the shower. The mole was still there. She rubbed it with her towel. Remembering how the old woman in the pool had looked at her, she wondered if it was some kind of surveillance device. The lump in her mouth had been removed, but she was sure they'd left some way of keeping track of her.

There was a pair of nail scissors beside the sink. She picked them up. The mole protruded from her skin enough for her to cut it off. Would she be allowed to change her body now that it didn't belong to her? She looked in the mirror. The mole stood out like a black spot, marking her for something.

She snipped it off. It didn't hurt as much as she expected, as if it had been slightly numbed. She put the scissors down as it started to bleed. Blood poured down her arm and onto the bathroom floor. She put a wad of tissue to it. Immediately it was soaked through. Sitting on the edge of the bathtub, she used one of her swimming towels. The stains would never come out. Soon the blood soaked through the towel. It seemed like too much blood. The pain grew to a deep ache. She had bandages in her cupboard. She took one out and peeled off the adhesive backing. She stuck it over where the mole had been, and then covered it with another. Spots of blood bloomed on the surface but didn't run over. She put the bloody towel in the washing machine and cleaned the bathroom floor with tissues, relieved that it was done.

TWO WEEKS LATER, Ada and her mother took the ferry from Athens to Naxos. It was just starting to get hot. Ada and her mother had flown from London and spent the night in Athens in a hotel with a rooftop bar. They went up for a drink in the evening and watched the sun sink into the Acropolis from amongst an array of potted bamboo plants. Ada struggled to make conversation. She heard her mother talking but couldn't make out the words. On the ferry she sat beside the window and looked at the ocean. There were no clouds in the sky. Ada hadn't told anyone that she'd left. Patrick hadn't contacted her again. She knew that he probably thought she wasn't interested in him, or that he'd offended her. She had tried to forget about

Francesca. The restaurant was her world, but it no longer felt like it belonged to her. She wondered if Francesca and Carlo had slept together. Francesca wouldn't care if he was married. Ada didn't want to see them. She had called up the restaurant the day after and quit. Francesca had called her twice since then, but she hadn't picked up.

On the ferry she wondered if she was lonely. It didn't feel the same as the loneliness she'd felt before the change. She wasn't waiting for anyone. She could swim in the sea and sunbathe all day, and nobody would know where she was or what she was doing. She had plans with her mother to visit some ancient ruins. They were staying in the small house close to the sea, just outside a village with a large harbor.

"I hope you'll go out and meet some people," her mother said. It was the last thing Ada wanted to do. She realized that although she had somehow expected her to, her mother didn't understand what had happened. Ada didn't know how to explain it. She only knew that she didn't want to go out and meet people.

Her mother was sitting on the deck. She wore a large pair of sunglasses. She had tried to persuade Ada to sit outside with her, but Ada wanted to be away from the hot sun and the too-blue ocean. Inside the boat, the air-conditioning made her cold, and the windows were slightly tinted. She felt cold all the way through. I have a cold heart, she thought.

The ferry dropped them on the other side of the island from where they were staying. Ada's mother wanted to eat lunch in a restaurant.

"I love it here," she said. "I used to come here when I was young."

They found a restaurant on the waterfront with stiff white tablecloths. Ada's mother put her bags under the table as they sat down. Neither of them had brought much. They ordered from a smartly dressed waiter.

"How're we going to get to the house?" Ada asked.

"I rented a car."

Ada looked around the harbor. She could see where the boat had come in. Smaller boats lined the semicircle of brick wall that divided them from the ocean. Some had people sunbathing on them, although it was early in the tourist season, or eating lunch. The water was sparkling blue and green. There were no trees. Behind the town, scrubland rose up into a series of rocky and uneven hills that made Ada think of ancient battles. Groups of people, Greek and foreign, walked backwards and forwards through the open space between the restaurants and the water.

"We should go swimming straightaway when we get there," her mother said. All Ada wanted to do was lie down and go to sleep. She had expected leaving everything behind to be enlivening, an opportunity to discover who she was now. Instead, she was filled with a dull and sluggish exhaustion that dragged her down.

"What do you want to do this evening?" she asked her mother.

"We'll go out. We can't sit around the house on our first night." The food arrived. They had ordered small plates to share. Ada's mother used a serving spoon to decant salad onto Ada's plate. "I hope you're going to keep me company," she said. Ada knew that she could already sense that something was wrong and was trying to avert it, letting Ada know that whatever it was would not be accepted.

"I'm just not feeling very well," Ada said. "I'm sorry." Her mother didn't say anything. Instead, she turned away to look at the view. The sharp, linear expression on her face spoke to a clenched jaw. Ada felt unhappiness well up inside her. She wondered if she had made the right decision in accepting the new body. In the moment it had felt like the answer to everything, a chance at a new, more secure way of being, but seeing Francesca and Carlo had brought the feelings that had momentarily dissipated straight back—her loneliness, her desperation to be loved. They rose again in the presence of her mother, a restless, choppy sea of discomfort.

She knew her lethargic mood would make her mother angry if it went on any longer, but she didn't know what to do to feel different. Explaining what had happened was impossible, but she knew that without an explanation things would be worse. Her mother would think her ungrateful and uncooperative. There was no way that Ada could tell her how badly things had gone wrong.

Her arm still hurt where she had cut off the mole. Her mother silently paid the bill, and they went to find the rental car. Her brisk movements told Ada she was already dissatisfied. Although Ada tried to make conversation, it was slow and stilted. For some reason she had always found it hard to ask her mother questions. When they found the rental office—a low, beige building with a large plastic sign and the same tinted windows as the ferry—her mother went inside without a word. Ada waited outside. It took a long time. Eventually she came back out with the car keys in her hand. Behind the office was a parking lot full of identical cars.

Ada's mother drove the car around to the front of the office. When Ada climbed in the front beside her, she stopped the engine.

"What's the matter with you?"

"Nothing," Ada said.

"I spent a lot of money to bring you here," her mother said. "You could at least pretend to be enjoying yourself."

"I'm tired," Ada said. "I'm sorry. I have a lot going on." Her mother started the engine again.

The drive took them across the middle of the island. The roads were steep, and the sharp corners difficult to maneuver. They went through a small village with a brilliant white church overlooking the steep hillside, like a single tooth in an old, decaying mouth. Everything was closed, and the village was silent and empty.

"Isn't that beautiful," her mother said, whenever they caught sight of the sea. The white froth left by the boats carrying tourists back and forth looked exactly like airplane trails in the blue sky. Ada felt that everything was turning upside down as they drove back down towards the sea, the car covered in dust.

When they reached the house, Ada got out to unload the bags. It was up a path only accessible by foot. Small purple flowers grew in between the cracked tiles. A fig tree hung over the gate, and the smell followed Ada as she walked towards the house. The house itself was low and crooked, built on uneven ground. It was dark inside. One single light bulb hung from the ceiling of each room. In the kitchen, long shelves held dusty brass pans and long skewers that looked as though they were for roasting animals over an open flame. Ada wondered how old they were. In the cupboards were plastic bowls and plates, and cups decorated with cartoon characters.

Ada's room was at the back. She sat down on the bed. The room had a window, covered by a screen to keep mosquitoes out, that looked over the overgrown courtyard. She could hear her mother moving things around. Whenever they arrived somewhere, her mother would rearrange the furniture, at least in the bedroom she was sleeping in. She liked to have her bed far away from the window, as any light kept her awake. Sometimes she brought her own blinds with her, made of heavy material that let nothing through. Sometimes she slept with a pillow over her face. She always woke up very early. Ada remembered listening to her creep around the house for hours before the sun rose, like a ghost.

Outside the window the sky was blue. Ada checked her phone. She had no messages. Her mother was waiting for her to go to the beach. She opened her suitcase and took out her towel. She hadn't brought many things. You have to make decisions, she thought, to be free. It doesn't come naturally.

She went downstairs to where her mother was waiting, standing on the cracked tiles of the courtyard.

"Are you ready?" she asked.

"Yes," Ada said.

"I don't understand why you were in such a bad mood on the journey."

"It was nothing," Ada said. "I didn't feel well."

"You're with me now. It's important for us to spend time together. We've been too separate recently." Her face was tight, as if speaking took more effort than usual. Ada wondered for a moment what would happen if she told her about the body. They were separate in a more fundamental way than her mother could possibly know—the biological bond between them had been broken. Ada felt a momentary swell of relief. Who else that she knew could say that? She had achieved individuality.

"We're not separate people," her mother said, sometimes. "We're two halves of the same brain." Ada always felt that she was overcompensating because the opposite was truer than it should've been. Her mother had often felt like a stranger to her, an unfamiliar presence who she had adapted to, rather than somebody tied to her by blood.

The beach was a ten-minute walk away, along the track, and then down steep cobbled steps that led through the heart of the village. Flowering bougainvillea hung from the white plastered walls. Ada thought that she had never seen anything so beautiful. She wanted to take a picture, but now that Atticus was gone, she had nobody to send it to. They turned a corner and the water appeared below them, flat as a mirror. Instead of a beach, there was a ladder down from the narrow street to a platform carved into the rock where you could jump into the water. Nobody else was there. They laid their towels out on the rough concrete. The dark blue color of the water told them it was deep. Ada's mother climbed down the rusty ladder ahead of her.

Ada wondered if the man in the white coat was watching her. She changed into her swimsuit on the platform, holding her towel around herself. Her mother was already in the water. Standing on the edge of the platform, the fear of the water that Ada had felt with Patrick beside the pool came back to her. She imagined her body covered in red rust like the ladder.

"Aren't you getting in?" her mother asked.

"I will," Ada said. She stood frozen on the platform. If she didn't swim, her mother would be angry. She imagined her mother watching as she sank down to the bottom, limbs jerking as the wiring inside her became saturated with salty water. A lizard ran across the concrete. "I don't know if I want to swim," she called to her mother.

Her mother swam away without replying. Her body made a triangle of ripples that reminded Ada of an arrowhead.

Ada jumped into the water. It rushed up her nose, and she tasted salt in the back of her mouth. Nothing happened. When she came up, she saw her mother treading water.

"It's nice," Ada said. Her mother didn't say anything. "What's wrong?"

"You could at least make an effort to talk to me," her mother said.

"I am talking to you."

"You were silent the whole walk down. I feel like I've brought you all the way here and you're not making any effort to talk to me."

"I'm sorry."

"You're acting like something is very wrong," her mother said. Her head sat on the surface of the water like a tennis ball. "I'm worried about you."

"Nothing's wrong." Ada was beginning to feel tired of treading water.

"What's happened?"

"Nothing. It was just working at the restaurant. It got too much."

"I thought you loved it there."

"I did. I just think I needed a change of scene."

Ada swam back to the rocks. She climbed back up the rusty ladder and sat on the platform with her towel wrapped around her shoulders. It was late in the day. She could feel her mother watching her, but she pretended not to notice. She looked out over the ocean. The water shifted uneasily beneath the reddening sun. Even the smallest waves threw up shadows. In the distance she could see the silhouette of another island, low and dark, like a hand resting flat against the water.

Her mother got out of the water. As she climbed the ladder, Ada tried to imagine what it was like to be her. Before, it had been easy. She knew that her mother was terrified of losing her, and she knew what she had to do to placate those fears. Now it was like Ada couldn't predict how her behavior would make her mother feel. She didn't know what it was like to be somebody else. In severing the link with Atticus, the doctor had severed her link to everyone. Now it was only the inside of her own mind stretching itself over everything, like a ceiling built so high up that for all intents and purposes it may as well have been the sky.

BACK AT THE house she got changed for dinner. They were going to another small restaurant that her mother claimed to know well.

"The owner is Russian," her mother said, on the walk back up. "I've told him all about you. Every time I go, he asks me when I'm going to bring him my daughter. I think it's the only thing he can say in English. He just says, 'Daughter, daughter,' over and over again."

There was a mirror in Ada's room. Her reflection was illuminated by a single light bulb. The walls were decorated with paintings of unclothed, nymphic women. Ada wondered how her mother had found the house. Their stay was open-ended.

When Ada went downstairs her mother was waiting on the patio, wearing a black shirt with a chain of red interlocking circles that faded in color as the chain progressed. Ada could see her collarbones, each cupping a pool of shadow. Her smooth blonde hair was arranged in a series of descending curls. The smell of the fig tree followed them as they walked down the path towards the village.

"Have you talked to your father recently?" her mother asked.

"No. He never calls me first."

"I can't believe that," her mother said. "He's totally abandoned you."

"I don't feel abandoned," Ada said. "He wants to talk to me, but he doesn't know how to."

"But you don't want to talk to him," her mother said.

"I do want to talk to him."

Her mother looked straight ahead at the path in front of them. The lights of the village appeared as they turned a corner. Ada sensed her mother crying, but she didn't want to look over and see. After a while, her mother said, "You wouldn't want to talk to him if you knew what I know."

Ada remained silent.

"I hate him," her mother said. "I hate him. You're better off without him."

There was a bench to one side of the path, coated in dust from the gravel path. Her mother sat down on it abruptly. Her face was white. Ada looked at the olive trees that stood on the other side of the path. They were barely taller than she was. In the darkness, they looked like humanoid figures. She imagined rows of twisted faces concealed in the leaves, all staring out at her. One by one, she imagined reaching in and gouging out their eyes. Her mother was still crying.

"I'm sorry," Ada said. She felt that she had done something terrible. Her mother stood up again and walked away.

Eventually they reached the restaurant. Ada's mother sat silently at the table, staring at the blue-and-white checked tablecloth. She didn't respond to the tall, blond waiter when he asked her what she wanted. Ada ordered for them both, shakily, knowing that what she was asking for was too much. Neither of them would eat anything now. They sat on the terrace, overlooking the small harbor. Ada's mother always wanted to eat outside. There was music playing from inside the restaurant.

"I wish you would say something," Ada said.

"What do you want me to say?"

"It's horrible sitting in silence."

Her mother gave a brief, harsh laugh. It sounded to Ada like the bark of a dog.

"You could try asking me a question."

"I do ask you questions," Ada said.

"No, you don't," her mother said. "You don't want me to be honest because you're scared of what you'll find out. If you did ask me what really happened, you would know that your father destroyed us."

"He didn't destroy me," Ada said. Part of her knew that her mother was right. She didn't want to ask questions. She didn't want to know whatever awful things had happened between them. There was a pressure in her head. She felt any movement would burst it open.

"How can you say that," her mother said, "when you don't even know what happened." Her face was tight. "You're like a completely different person."

"That's not true," Ada said. Her mother was the only person who had noticed. Ada wondered if that was why she'd agreed to the holiday. She had known that her mother would sense that something had changed. Ada wished to tell her that she was right, to seal the gap back up. The waiter passed nearby, and for a moment neither of them spoke. The nausea suddenly worsened, and Ada wondered if she would be sick.

"I know what's going on," her mother said. Her voice was like the tolling of a high, clear bell. "I can hear your father speaking through you. I tried to show you how cruel he is, but you were never interested in what I had to say, and now I've lost you."

"That's not what's happening. I just want to be honest."

"Honesty is overrated," her mother said. "You're selfish. You only care about men. If you loved me as much as you seem to love your father, none of this would be happening."

"I do love you," Ada said.

"No, you don't," her mother said.

Ada imagined the white room. It was inside her somewhere, she thought, a space that she could escape to.

The waiter brought their food. Ada stood up and left the table. Her mother said her name, sharply, but she pretended not to hear. She walked away from the restaurant, across the square that separated them from the harbor wall. It was dark, but warm yellow light danced from the windows of the low, white houses. A sultry breeze blew up off the black ocean, more like tar than air. Ada passed the line of bars that faced out onto the water. The tourist season hadn't quite begun, and some of them were closed, chairs chained together and stacked up in geometric piles. She climbed over the low wall that separated the street from the beach. The tide was out, revealing black, sulphuric rocks, covered in seaweed that slipped around beneath her feet. Everything was unraveling. For the first time in her life, she wondered if her mother really loved her.

She sat down on the beach. The ground was wet and smelled strongly of fish and salt. In the far distance she could see the lights of the next island. The stretch of water between them was deep and cold. Ada imagined creatures moving beneath the waves. She remembered that Atticus's father was Greek. It was possible he came from the same island, maybe even the same town, that she and her mother were visiting. Any of the houses lining the inner curve of the square could have been his father's home. As a child he could have sat on the very beach where she was now sitting.

There was something wet on her neck. Touching it with her fingers, she wondered if it was blood. There wasn't enough light to see clearly. She wiped her hand on her white shirt and nothing came away, but it kept trickling down her neck in a small stream. With her fingers she followed it up to the base of her skull. Her hairline was damp. She tried to stem the flow but it ran over her hand and down her arm. It was only when she moved her head forwards that she felt a long, narrow crack open up in the back of her skull. It was leaking salt water. Ada remembered jumping into the ocean. The water must have found its way into the body and corroded her from the inside, and now she was splitting open.

What could she do? Briefly she thought about killing herself. Was the man watching her? Someone walked past her in the dark, or she thought they did, and she flinched away from them. She took out her phone. It was just past ten. She called her father.

"Ada?" he always pronounced her name *Ay-da*, rather than the *Ah-da* that her mother preferred.

"Is this a good time?"

"I can talk for five minutes." It sounded like he was in the car.

"I'm not feeling very well." She began to cry.

"Where are you?"

"I'm in Greece with Mum. We've had a fight." She heard him exhale.

"I didn't know you'd gone on holiday." He paused. "I can't get involved in your relationship with your mother. It's between you and her. You can't not tell me you've gone on holiday and then ring me up and expect me to fix it."

"I know." She didn't know what to say. She felt embarrassed for having called him.

"Call me if you need anything," he said. "You'll be okay." He hung up.

The flow of water seemed to have stopped. Ada felt around at the base of her neck. The crack started behind her right ear and ran upwards diagonally. It wasn't painful. She looked for something to cover it with, but she'd left her jacket in the restaurant. The air had started to cool down. Somewhere in the dark, the sea moved in and out. It sounded like somebody breathing. She looked up, and the sky was full of stars. As she looked into the black emptiness between them, she felt she was looking into herself. She was made of cosmic emptiness, of swirling dust and rocks, of voids that ate everything. Even the round, glowing moon did not reach out its arms to embrace her, but looked impassively away. Help me, she thought.

She felt a wave of prickling anticipation that ran up and down the length of her body, as if she had just been told something exciting but didn't know what. As the white room appeared around her, she realized it had been there the whole time, folded up infinitesimally small in the corner of her vision. She was sitting on the sofa. After she had been waiting for a while, the man came in.

"I didn't expect you to actually respond," she said. "I didn't know that you could hear me."

"We can hear everything," he said.

"I want it to be reversed," she said. "I want my body back."

"It's not possible. The change is permanent."

"It's cracking apart."

"I know," he said. "I'm sorry."

"Why isn't it working?" Ada asked.

"I think maybe what we set out to do simply isn't feasible. Human beings are not designed to experience themselves in isolation. We wanted you to be free, but really we just ensured that you were alone. It's cracking because it can't withstand the pressure."

"Are you just going to abandon me?" Ada started to panic.

"No. I think it would be best if you came and stayed with us." Ada looked at him. His face was grave. He looked older.

"I'm sorry," he said. "We made a terrible mistake."

"What will my family do?"

"We can arrange something. We can send another version of you down, one that has no memory of what happened."

"You have another version of me?"

"We built it in case things went wrong."

"In case I died?"

The man didn't say anything. He was looking down at the surface of the table. Ada looked around the room. It was like she was seeing it for the first time. "I do feel like I belong here," she said. There was silence between them. "Where did you come from?" she asked.

"Somewhere very far away."

"Is that where I'll go? Where you came from?"

"No. You'll stay here. It has everything you'll need. It stretches for hundreds of miles. You won't get bored." She nodded. It was a nice idea. There was something comforting about the idea of retreat—she could give up without having to lose herself fully. She could immerse herself in something completely different. "We all look like you. We eat the same food as you. You can live amongst us. You don't have to be alone."

"It's like heaven," she said. The man laughed. "What will happen if you decide to leave?"

"We won't," he said. "We really do want to help you."

"Okay," she said. It seemed like the right thing to say. The thought of going back to the beach made her shiver. "Does it have to happen now?"

"No," the man said. "You can go back down if you want."

"I have a question," she said. He nodded, indicating that she should ask. "Why did I see the visions of Atticus?"

"What do you mean?"

"I saw him, after he went back to California. It was like I was in the room with him, but he couldn't see me, and I couldn't move. Sometimes it felt like I was becoming him."

"That wasn't us," he said. "I'm not sure what you're talking about."

"But you know everything," she said. "You can hear my thoughts."

"Maybe you were dreaming," he said. "We don't look at your dreams."

SUDDENLY SHE WAS back on the beach. It was abrupt. She'd closed her eyes in one place and opened them in the other. There was a cold wave moving around in her stomach. The first thing she thought of was Atticus and whether the visions she had of him had been a dream. The world around her seemed to slant and stretch. She got to her feet and brushed the sand and seaweed from her clothes. Her trousers were wet from sitting on the damp sand.

She found her way back to the harbor wall. The bars were still silent and closed, the tables and chairs still stacked in tall piles, and the awnings rolled up. The restaurant where she and her mother had been sitting was empty. She looked at her phone. Several hours had passed, although it had felt like only a few minutes. Her mother must have gone back to the house. It was very dark. She started walking back the way they had come, along the road that led out of the village and into the silent countryside.

As she walked, she thought about the offer the man had made her. She wondered if he had really swapped her body for a replacement, or if it had been an experiment on a deeper level, to see if they could get her to believe it. The last house of the village passed her. The moon, nearly full, bathed her surroundings in watery light. She only had to walk up the hill, past the olive trees, and she would reach the house. She stumbled over a rock. There was a pain in her chest. She didn't know how she would apologize to her mother. She wanted to leave knowing that they were on good terms. Her mother was all she had.

The moon was bright enough that it reflected off the chalky path, turning it into a white river. The gate came into sight. The lights in the house were off. Presumably, her mother had gone to sleep. As Ada opened the front door, she was suddenly afraid that her mother wouldn't be there, that she would go upstairs and find both the bedrooms empty. The pain in her chest deepened. It was an ache, as if she had been struck by a blunt object. Things seemed to spin around her. She struggled to find the light switch. The wall was smooth under her hands. She made her way up the stairs in the dark, afraid of tripping over something. When she reached the top, she could see more clearly—moonlight came in through a partially open window. She found the door of her bedroom and opened it. She turned the lights on, but the light was dim. There was somebody in her bed. It was her mother, asleep. The sheet was pulled up over her face, as if she were a dead body. Ada remembered how, as a child, she would go to her mother's room and pull back the sheet from her face to bring her back to life.

IN THE EARLY morning, there was a storm. When Ada woke up it hadn't yet started to rain and there was a strange silence outside of the hammering thunder, as if it had cracked open the sky, and all the other sound had fallen in. Lightning flashed outside the window. It occurred instantaneously with the thunder. Ada remembered being told that it meant they were right beneath the heart of it.

It started to rain. Ada got up without turning on the light and looked out the window. She could see the olive trees whipping themselves and the plants in the garden lying flat against the ground. Blue light was just beginning to dilute the sky. Ada pictured the raging, thrashing ocean slamming itself against the low coastline. If the tide came in, the boats in the harbor would be smashed to pieces.

She felt something on her face and stepped away from the window. Rain found its way through the unstable casing and soaked both sides of the dirty glass. Ada was in her mother's room. Her mother's suitcase was open on the floor beside the bed. It was empty. All the clothes were piled on an armchair in the corner. Ada turned on the light and looked through them. Her mother liked bright colors. She was from Leeds and said that they were the only antidote to the gray northern sky. Looking through the clothes, Ada found all of them ugly, like the upholstery of bad furniture. The storm shook the pictures on the walls. Ada got back into her mother's bed and lay awake until the sky was light and everything was quiet.

When she went downstairs, it was already hot and the sun had burned the water from the patio. Her mother was sitting at the wooden table in the kitchen. She was wearing a pink shirt, and her blonde hair was tied up in a bun. Ada could see the tattoo on the back of her neck, a small sun with lines radiating outwards.

Ada came in and said good morning. She sat down at the table beside her mother.

"How're you feeling?" her mother asked.

"I'm okay," Ada said. She was hungry but she didn't want to say it, afraid to remind her mother of what had happened.

"Let's just forget about last night," her mother said. Her face was placid and calm. "We can have a nice day today."

Birds were singing outside the window, and she could hear the rustle of wind in the olive trees. Her mother looked straight ahead at the whitewashed wall, where copper pans hung from a railing above the stove.

"Did you hear the storm?" Ada asked.

"No," her mother said.

"It was this morning," Ada said. "It rocked the whole house."

"I don't know what you're talking about," her mother said. Ada looked at her. There was something different about her.

"Should we go to the beach?" Ada asked.

"I already went this morning, before you woke up."

"What should we do instead?"

"I think we should drive up the hill and look at the church."

"Okay," Ada said.

Her mother smiled. Ada wondered if the smile was real. There was a sharp pain in her stomach, and a dull ache at the base of her skull.

She went upstairs to get ready. In the bathroom, she looked at her body in the mirror. There was a circular red scab where the mole had been. If she narrowed her eyes she could almost see her fourteen-year-old self, rigid and upright as the mast of a ship.

The crack in the back of her head had closed up. If she pressed down hard enough, she could feel a seam, as if the edges had been sewn back together.

As she turned away from the mirror, something caught her eye. Her back looked like she'd fallen into a bush of thorns. It was covered in thin, raised scratches, some of which had bled in the night and stained her shirt. She looked down at her hands. Beneath her fingernails were crescents of red. Taking off the stained shirt, she wondered why her mother hadn't said anything. In her bedroom she changed into new clothes.

Downstairs her mother was waiting for her. They got in the car.

"We could stop for a coffee," Ada said. It was the sort of thing that her mother liked to do.

"Let's see if we find somewhere with a view."

Her mother started the car. Ada felt that she was out of reach, locked away behind a thick glass door.

"I've been having terrible dreams," Ada said. Her mother didn't answer for a moment. She was wearing large sunglasses, and Ada couldn't make out her expression without turning around fully to look at her. She imagined the car going off the road and tearing through the olive trees, plunging over a cliff and diving into the sparkling sea.

"What happens in them?"

"I become somebody else."

"Who?"

"A man I met. I don't really know him. He was staying in my building."

"Did you have a relationship with him?"

"No." There was silence. Ada knew she was making things worse. With every bump of the car on the uneven road, she felt the pain in her stomach and worried that she'd split open again. "I'm sorry," she said.

"You hurt me very deeply last night," her mother said. "When I was a child, I thought nobody would love me until I had children of my own. Now I'm beginning to think I've done everything wrong. We should have been more like friends. You can't count on family to want you. It's better if they love you because they like who you are."

"Do you like who I am?"

"I don't know who you are."

They drove on in silence. When they reached the church, they got out of the car. They were in a small village of no more than ten houses, all the same color as the gray rocks and all crumbling into the dust. The church stood on a square of paved ground with nothing around it. It was painted white. The structure itself was unremarkable—it was cubic and solid, with a stunted tower rising up from the center. No bell hung in the belfry. Ada and her mother approached the door. It was thick and unpainted. Ada expected it to be locked, but the large brass door handle turned easily. It was dark in the church. Ada followed her mother inside. The space was larger than the outside of the building had suggested. It was cold, and smelled of incense and damp wood. Candles stood in a rack against one wall, arranged like singers in a choir. High in the ceiling was a window, barely two inches wide, that let in a single shaft of light. It fell above a large cross that loomed behind the altar, illuminating a square of the mildewed wall. On either side of the cross were paintings—one of the Madonna with the child Christ, and one of the Pietà, the Madonna supporting the lifeless, crucified body of her now-adult son.

In the center of the room was a wooden boat supported by a stone pedestal. It stood in the aisle, rows of chairs on either side. It was large, but not large enough to fit a person. The body was long and low. Oars stuck out along both sides, covered by a fishing net made of knotted string. Benches traversed the inner cavity. It was undecorated. A small sign was nailed to the wall, barely legible in the candlelight. It was in English. Ada's mother leaned in to read it.

"It's a model," she said. "Of the boats the villagers used to use to fish in the eighteen hundreds. They built it themselves." She walked around it, slowly. "Isn't it beautiful?"

"It reminds me of the boat from the house in France," Ada said. Ada and her parents had stayed in a house with a lake accessible through the garden. A wooden rowing boat, partially rotted, was available for their use. Ada, only ten, had spent days exploring the shaded banks of the lake. She had been enchanted by the pond skaters, light enough to suspend themselves on the surface of the water, and the crayfish, with their tiny lobster claws. She had bent so far over the water trying to see them that she had fallen in. Convinced that the crayfish would eat her, she had nearly drowned in her struggle to climb back into the boat.

"That was a good trip," her mother said.

Ada sat down on one of the chairs. The boat was at her eye level. She imagined the villagers building it. Had they done it from memory, or did they have a drawing? The more she looked at it, the more flaws appeared—it was roughly hewn, with splinters sticking up from the surface, and the oars were all different sizes. It was like each person had remembered a different boat and carved their own section from memory. The statue itself was an amalgamation of memories passed down through generations, assembled into something entirely new. It made Ada sad to look at it.

They left the church. Although they rarely touched, Ada was desperate for her mother to embrace her. Nobody had touched her since Patrick had tried. How can she not know who I am, Ada thought. She's been with me since I was born. It occurred to her that perhaps there was nothing within her to know.

On the way home, they stopped in the village. A café was open in the mess of cobbled streets behind the harbor. It had a faded green awning, where the name was written in Greek and in English. Ada was glad to be away from the harbor. They sat down at a table outside.

"Do you want to share something?" her mother asked. Her voice was clipped. "A pastry?" Ada nodded. She knew that if she spoke, she would cry. There was too much—the doctor's offer to remove her, the revelation that she had only dreamt of Atticus, her failure as a daughter and as a friend, as a person. Her mother's tentative kindness made it worse. Even the memory of the boat on the lake wasn't real—it had happened to somebody else. She had nothing. Her own mother didn't recognize her. Despite her best efforts, tears slipped through, running down her cheeks in two straight lines.

"Don't make that face," her mother said. "I'm trying my best not to be upset. You hurt me, not the other way around." Ada wiped her cheeks with a napkin. Could it be true? Was it she who had hurt her mother? It felt to Ada as if it was the other way around. The waiter brought two coffees and a pastry with a knife. Her mother cut the pastry in half. It was filled with dense cream. Her mother put the plate in front of Ada. Ada continued to cry. She could feel that something had shaken loose. Her mother no longer loved her, and love was all she wanted. Her mother looked away, embarrassed, waiting for her to stop. Eventually she stood up.

"Enough of this," she said. "We need to go home." Ada followed her along the cobbled streets. The air smelled strongly of oranges and the window baskets of the houses were full of small white flowers. Ada followed blindly, passing the stalls of colorful souvenirs without noticing or knowing where they were going. By the time they reached the house only the tears that still poured down her wet cheeks indicated that something lived below the surface. "This is ridiculous," her mother said. "You're acting like an insane person."

Ada stood in the middle of her room, unable to move. Everything inside her had dissolved into a black, empty void. Her sobs turned into a scream. Her mother stood by the door as she screamed and screamed. It was the worst pain Ada had ever felt, worse than when she'd fallen down the stairs and broken her wrist. It was like being torn in half. I am nothing, she thought. Nothing, nothing, nothing. It reverberated through her like an echo. If nobody loves me, I am nothing.

Part 3

Ada rarely left her room. It scared her to go out amongst the people—if that was what they were. Anything she asked for was brought to her door. Meals were delivered by a woman in a white apron. Ada didn't know where the food came from. She had never seen a kitchen. Were they close enough to Earth to receive deliveries? Did they grow the vegetables themselves? She asked the woman, but the woman just laughed, as if she didn't know what Ada was talking about.

What disturbed Ada was that she could ask for anything. If she wanted a steak, it would appear at her door within minutes. She tried asking for things with strange, exotic ingredients, bamboo fungus and fermented fish, that surely they would not have on hand, and always it appeared just as quickly. Long-aged cheese, slow-cooked stews, flash-fried chicken, macaroni and white sauce specifically from a packet were all presented to her by the woman, who never appeared hurried or flustered. She knocked quietly, twice, and smiled when Ada opened the door. The plates came covered in metal domes to keep the heat in, and after placing the trays on Ada's desk the woman would remove them with a flourish that contained something of the theatrical, as if she was proud of what she was presenting, and wanted Ada to know.

They rarely talked. Ada submitted her orders through a telephone beside her bed, like calling room service in a hotel. There was no voice on the other end. The only thing the woman ever said was, "How are you?" When Ada said that she was well, the woman would smile warmly and go away. Once Ada had replied with, "I'm well, how're you?" The woman had looked at her and said, "I wouldn't know how to describe it."

All Ada could think about was finding something that was impossible for them to serve her. She knew that it was ungrateful—they wanted to give her everything. There was no reason for her to stay in her room. There were miles of corridors to explore, hundreds of people to meet and talk to. On a whim, she had asked them to build her a swimming pool, but once it was completed, she never went to see it. Her room was comfortable. They had asked her if she'd like to change it in any way—she could have whatever she wanted—but she said that she liked it how it was. It had a narrow bed, a desk, a chair, and a wardrobe. She enjoyed feeling like a monk, or a prisoner. A large, clean bathroom, used by only her, was accessible through a door to the side. She wondered if she had offended them by refusing the full extent of their hospitality, but they never let it show.

One day she had an idea. She would ask them for a chocolate bar, still in the wrapper. There was no way they could manufacture a chocolate bar wrapper in two minutes. If they presented her with one, it was proof that they were receiving supplies from Earth—maybe that they were even on Earth, in some remote desert or arctic location where the facility would never be found. She picked up the phone. She didn't know what she'd do with the confirmation if she got the chocolate bar. She had no desire to escape and live in the world again. She was defective, like animals raised by humans, no longer recognizable by their own kind. She felt afraid of other people, more afraid of them than she was of the imitations who now surrounded her.

There was a low buzzing coming from the other end of the phone line.

"Snickers bar," she said. Then she waited.

She tried not to think about the other version of herself, the one that had picked up her life where she had dropped it. She pulled the bedcovers over her head. There were no windows in the facility, but the brightness given off by the ceiling lights was like daylight. They came on and off on a twelve-hour cycle. There were no switches, although Ada supposed she could ask for one to be installed. Once the lights had gone off for the night, she could use the lamp on her desk, which emitted a warm orange glow, but usually when it got dark, she climbed into bed and fell asleep instantly, waking up only when the false dawn broke above her head. She had terrible dreams in which a parade of the people she knew walked past her, shouting and screaming in her face. She couldn't move to get away or speak to defend herself. When she woke up, she was always tangled up in the bedsheets and couldn't go back to sleep until she'd stripped the bed and remade it. Sometimes she became convinced that somebody was about to come into her room and kill her and would sit up against the headboard with her eyes fixed on the door until the lights came on.

She heard a gentle knock. Ada climbed out of bed to answer it. She was wearing pale blue pajamas. All the clothes they had given her were pale blue. When she asked the man why, he said it was his favorite color. She asked, "Why not make them my favorite color?"

"What's your favorite color?" he'd asked.

"Red," she said. She'd selected it at random, realizing as she'd asked the question that she didn't have a favorite color.

"I'm sorry," he said. "I didn't know that. We can change them."

"Don't worry," she said. "I like the blue."

She opened the door. The woman stood there with a plate in her hand. On the plate was a wrapped Snickers bar. She came into Ada's room and put it down on the desk.

"How are you?" she asked.

"I'm okay," Ada said. She looked at the chocolate bar. The wrapping was perfect. It was just how she remembered it. "How did you make it?" she asked.

"What do you mean?" the woman said.

"Where did it come from?"

"It came from you wanting it," the woman said. "I wouldn't bring you something you didn't want."

"But how did you make it so perfectly?"

"I'm not sure I can explain it to you." The woman smiled. "I'm glad you think it's perfect."

"Does anything I imagine just appear?" Ada looked at the woman for a sign of frustration. She didn't want to be rude, but she felt that she needed to know. The woman's face was calm. There was a slightly amused curve to her lip.

"You could see it like that," she said.

"Why doesn't it just appear in my room?"

"Then I wouldn't have anything to do," the woman said.

She left, closing the door softly behind her. Ada felt strangely crushed. She didn't know how to want things. The Snickers bar sat on her desk, as appealing as a block of concrete. She picked it up. The packaging was smooth and crisp. The ingredients were listed on the back. Half of them were chemicals she'd never heard of. How could something she didn't know about come from her imagination? There had to be something else filling in the gaps. She read the fine print. It said all the usual things—satisfaction guaranteed, or your money back. Sugar should be consumed as part of a balanced diet. There was a number to call if the product was defective. She picked up the phone again and typed it in. To her surprise, it rang. A man answered.

"Hello?" he said. "Who is this?" He had an accent that Ada couldn't place.

"I don't like my Snickers bar," she said.

"I don't see what that has to do with me," the man said. "Is this some kind of a joke?"

"I have the wrong number," she said, and hung up. She looked back at the packet. The only thing she couldn't find was an expiration date.

She decided that she would spend the whole day in bed. She picked up the phone for the third time and ordered scrambled eggs. Although she had enjoyed cooking for herself back on Earth, she didn't miss it. Here it was easier to have things done for you. She wondered whose phone number had been on the Snickers bar. The man had sounded young. She wondered if she should call him back and warn him that his phone number was being distributed on chocolate bar wrappers. He had sounded surprised, so she assumed it hadn't happened before. She couldn't imagine many people called the number on their Snickers bar. It seemed like something only a crazy person would do. She called him back.

"Hello?" he said. "Hello?"

"It's me again," she said.

"Oh." He paused. "I can't help you with your chocolate bar."

"What's your name?"

"Darius." She was sure he was going to hang up, but he didn't.

"Your phone number was on my Snickers," she said. "You should probably change it."

"I think you dialed it wrong," he said. He had a high voice and sounded worried.

"Where are you?" she said.

"Poznań," he said.

"Where's that?"

"It's in Poland." He paused again but didn't hang up. "Where are you?"

"I don't know. How did you learn English?"

"I'm not speaking English," he said. "I'm speaking Polish."

There was a knock at the door, and she hung up.

THE CORRIDORS ALL looked the same. The temperature of the air felt the same as the temperature of her skin. It had been a few days since she had called Darius. She had hoped he would call her back, but he didn't. She was growing bored of being in bed and had gone for a walk.

She didn't know how long she'd been in the facility. It felt like it had been at least two months. There were no clocks or calendars. She wasn't sure that the others experienced time the same way she did. She had never seen any of them sleep, although she assumed that they did, since they had human bodies. It would be strange to eat but not to sleep. At night it was quiet—she rarely heard anyone in the corridor outside her room. The only person who she really talked to was the man who'd brought her there. He told her that his name was Don.

She wanted to find the swimming pool they'd built for her. It was at the end of a narrow corridor that looked like all the other corridors. No matter how far she wandered from her room she never seemed to get lost. It was like living in a hotel—she found that she always retained an awareness of where she was in relation to the things she knew. If she became disoriented, she closed her eyes and visualized the way back. Her visualizations were always correct.

The door to the pool was painted gray, but the paint had started to chip. She opened it. The pool wasn't like the one in her apartment block. It was a blank white square from which a section had been removed and filled with water. There were no loungers or changing rooms. Looking at it, she realized that she was disappointed. She had somehow expected them to know exactly how it was meant to be.

She stood at the edge, not sure of what to do. She was still wearing the blue pajamas and the thought of taking off her clothes in such an unfamiliar place made her uneasy. She sat down. Don had assured her on her arrival that they were no longer monitoring her thoughts, but she still felt wary, as if everyone around her could see inside her head. Not that she ever thought of very much. She put her feet in the water, soaking the bottom of the pajamas. She had another pair in her room. She had other clothes too, but she mostly wore the pajamas. They were comfortable and said nothing about her. The water was cooler than she'd expected. She lowered herself in, the pajamas floating around her in a blue cloud, and swam up and down before climbing out again. Her body was frail from weeks of inactivity, and even after the short swim she was out of breath. Her wet hair stuck to her face. She heard the door open behind her and turned around. It was Don. He still wore his doctor's uniform.

"Hello," he said. "Can I join you?" She nodded. He sat down beside her. Ada felt suspicious of him. How had he known she was there? It was possible that she was still being watched, monitored as part of an ongoing experiment, one they hadn't told her about.

"I saw you come in here from the corridor," he said. For a few minutes neither of them spoke. Ada watched the water ripple where she'd disturbed it. "Is there anything you want?" he said, eventually. "Or anything that we can do for you?"

"No," she said.

"I don't want you to be unhappy," he said.

"I'm not unhappy," Ada said. "I'm fine. I just don't want anything." He didn't believe her. She knew he wouldn't leave until she left herself, or she admitted that there was something she wanted, something that would make everything fall into place. "I called someone on the phone," she said.

"Who was it?"

"I called the customer satisfaction number on the Snickers bar. A man in Poland picked up. He said he was speaking Polish, but I heard him speaking English."

"The number must have been a misprint."

"How did I understand him?"

Don took a moment before answering, as if he didn't want to tell her.

"There wasn't someone on the other end. It was just what you imagined would happen, even if you didn't know it."

"Everything here happens on the inside," Ada said. "It's all about wanting things or imagining things. Nothing's real."

"It sounds like you don't take yourself very seriously, if you can't imagine that the things you want are real."

Ada pinched the wet fabric of her pajamas between her fingers. The strange, blank feeling grew stronger. She was just a pair of eyes. She stood up.

"It's not what I want," she said. "It's only what I ask for."

She left the room. Don didn't follow her. His words felt small and cold. When she got back to her room she climbed into bed and pulled the covers over her head.

THE BED WAS comfortable. The sheets were light, but she never got cold, and they never seemed to get dirty. They always felt fresh and crisp. Sometimes when she first woke up, she could forget where she was and pretend she was back in her studio apartment, although she had never remembered to wash her sheets back home, and they had always felt cold and damp. Remembering where she was came as a mixture of sadness and relief. Sometimes she lay in bed and thought about the people she had known dying one by one. It always made her feel better to picture it, like she was coughing up fluid from her lungs and could breathe more clearly afterwards.

She knew they didn't miss her. It was a relief to think about the other version of her, keeping them company. They didn't even know that she was gone. In the dark cave beneath her comforter, she imagined what she would say to her mother if she ever saw her again. She would apologize and try to explain everything. It had all been her fault. She had failed to live her life on her own terms.

The problem was she didn't know what it meant to live on her own terms. Had her life before not been her own? Nobody had ever asked her to do anything or expected anything of her, apart from simply being herself. She sat up in bed. The phone was beside her on the desk. She picked it up and dialed her father's number. It was the only one she knew by heart. It rang for a while, but nobody answered. She dialed the number from the Snickers bar, which still sat on her desk.

"Hello, Darius," she said, when she heard him pick up.

"Hello," he said, in his accented voice. "I don't know your name."

"I don't think I have a name."

"That's okay," he said. There was a pause. "Why are you calling me?"

"I thought you might want to talk. I thought you might be lonely."

"I am lonely." He said it simply, with no hint of sadness in his voice.

"What's it like in Poznań?"

"It's a beautiful city with a river running all the way through it."

"What did you do today?" Ada was looking at the white wall. She wished that there were a window.

"On the tree outside the window there are two squirrels. They come most days. Sometimes they talk to each other in a loud chatter that I can hear from my bedroom." He paused. "When I woke up, I knew that somebody had died. For a moment I thought that it was me. I listened to the squirrels running up and down the branches. When they dislodged an acorn, it fell on the roof. The acorns fell one after another, as if somebody was standing up there hitting the slats with a tiny hammer. As I listened, I wondered what my life would be like now that I was dead. My body would continue to move around without me. It was very dark outside, and I realized that I hadn't opened my eyes. When I opened them, I realized it wasn't me who was dead. It was my father. He had died in his sleep."

"What was he like?"

"I don't know. He's very fat. He was a lawyer. Now he sits around and watches television. I go to his flat, and we watch it together."

"That doesn't sound so bad."

"It's not. I just wish he had something to do before he died. If he had a dog, it could keep him company, and he would have had to go outside to take it on walks. They could walk along the river. He might have lived longer."

"Why didn't you get him one?" Ada asked.

"I was worried he wouldn't look after it."

"That's sad," Ada said. "That you didn't think he would."

"Some people aren't good at taking care of living things."

"That's true." Ada sat in silence. She couldn't hear Darius breathing on the other end of the phone, but it didn't disturb her. It was nice just to know that he was there. "Tell me more about yourself," she said.

"I want to be a photographer," he said. "But I'm worried about money."

"What do you do now?"

"I'm a real estate agent." Now that he wasn't so worried, his voice was quiet and calm. Ada felt that she could tell him anything. She felt that she loved him.

"What would you take photographs of?"

"Animals," he said. "I love animals. That's why I couldn't get the dog."

After a while Ada hung up the phone. It occurred to her that she could make up as many people as she wanted. Through the telephone she could build a whole world. She could be anybody. She imagined herself expanding like a balloon. She got out of bed and went into the corridor. She had no idea what time of day it was—she had given up trying to keep track of it. There was nobody around. She went back into her room and picked up the phone. Sitting at the desk, she imagined Atticus on the other end of it, and dialed a random number.

"Hello?" his voice was warm and deep, just as she remembered it.

"It's Ada," she said.

"It's good to hear from you," he said. "I've been thinking about you since we stopped communicating."

"You used my memories for your novel, but they don't belong to you. They're mine."

"I didn't mean to. I admire you a lot. I thought you wouldn't mind."

"I don't admire you," she said. "I think you're embarrassing."

THE NEXT MORNING, she was woken up by a knock at her door. She opened it, expecting the woman, but it was Don. He said that he wanted to show her something.

It took them a long time to get there. Don led her down what felt like miles of identical corridors. Soon she was lost. The only thing she knew was that they were going up. They climbed what seemed like endless flights of narrow stairs, all covered in soft white fabric. Ada imagined a window at the very top, through which she would be able to see the stars. She hadn't worn her shoes and her feet left shallow imprints, as if beneath the carpet, the floor was made of gel.

Eventually they reached a door. Don didn't open it immediately.

"Do you like it here?" he asked.

"Yes," Ada said. "I love it."

"If you see what I'm about to show you, you can't go back."

"I didn't realize I could anyway."

Don opened the door, and they stepped through. The space opened up, and for a moment Ada thought they were standing outside. They were standing on a narrow platform built into the interior wall of a column that rose up as far as Ada could see. She leaned forwards and looked over the edge, where it fell away into darkness. The space was so wide that Ada could barely make out the shadow of another platform and another door on the far wall.

In the center of the column hung a transparent oblong made of what looked at first like purple light. It shifted restlessly as Ada watched it, filling the center of the column, fluid and somehow alive. It reminded Ada of water or smoke, but it wasn't exactly either—it was more like liquid glass. Although it appeared insubstantial, she was sure that if she tried to touch it she would feel the presence of some kind of mass.

"Everything for us is the opposite of what it is for you," Don said. "In there is the outside. Everything around us is the inside, populated by our imaginations. How you think of things is how they are."

"I don't understand." Ada stared at the shape. It was like looking into deep water. There were things in it, objects that she couldn't make out. For a moment she thought she glimpsed herself.

"Imagine you peel an orange," Don said. "When you've removed the peel, you scrunch it up so that the white part is on the outside and the skin is compressed together on the inside."

"Where are your bodies?" Ada asked.

"In there," Don said, looking into the shape.

"It's like living in a dream." Ada stood on the edge of the platform and looked down. She had never seen anything so deep. She imagined rows of bodies hung neatly like coats on a clothes rail. "What happens if I jump off?" she asked.

"I don't know," Don said. "Whatever you think will happen."

Ada imagined herself suspended in midair. She stepped forwards. There was nothing beneath her feet, but she didn't fall. She looked back at Don.

"Why did you give me a fake body?" she asked.

"Bodies are just houses." He was looking down into the pit below them. "We wanted to make what was on the inside more real. We wanted to make it the same for you as it is for us, swapping the inside and the outside."

"The last thing I needed," Ada said, "was for all my thoughts to be real." She imagined herself falling, and instantly the platform disappeared. Wind rushed past her. She could fall forever and never hit the bottom. She thought about falling into bed, the soft covers reaching up to envelop her. She closed her eyes and pictured it. When she opened them, she was in her room. Her bed was warm. There was a knock at the door. She got up and opened it, expecting Don, but it was the woman, a tray in her hand.

SHE CALLED DARIUS.

"Have you remembered your name?" he asked.

"Ada," she said.

"Why didn't you tell me before?"

"I didn't want to."

"I understand," he said. "Sometimes I don't want to be myself." He paused. "Tell me about Ada."

"There's nothing to tell."

"Then I'll tell you more about myself. I'll tell you about my great-grandfather. I was just thinking about him. He lived in Poznań when the Germans took it over. He joined their side by choice. He wanted to be one of them."

"That's awful," Ada said.

"He wanted to save his family," Darius said. "That's what my grandfather said."

"Did he regret it?"

"He wouldn't speak about it. I met him once when I was a small child, and he scared me. When he was very old, he was prosecuted. I never learned the details. It may be that he worked in a camp. If he did, he volunteered. He died before the court date. I've always worried that I have evil in my soul, passed down from him."

Ada touched her face, pretending it was his.

"It's not your fault," she said.

"When I was a child, I killed a mouse," Darius said. "Afterwards I realized it was his spirit possessing me, the spirit of evil. I couldn't believe what I'd done. Since then, I've been worried that it'll come back."

"You're not evil," Ada said. "All children do things like that."

"I know that," Darius said. "I just needed someone to forgive me, but I was too afraid to tell anybody."

"When I was ten," Ada said, "I climbed out of my bedroom window. It was on the top floor. My neighbor saw me and knocked on the front door to tell my parents."

"What happened next?"

"I told them I was trying to catch a spider. I think they knew I wanted to scare them." Ada lapsed into silence. She could hear Darius breathing on the other end of the line. "What does it feel like to be possessed by the spirit of evil?" she asked.

"On the outside everything is the same, but you know that the people around you are all wearing masks, and underneath the mask they want to hurt you. Then you hurt them to defend yourself, but afterwards you realize that none of it was real, and you were the one wearing the mask." He paused. "I was sitting in the garden and I felt a shadow fall over me. I looked up, but there was nothing there. On the grass there was a mouse that the neighbor's cat had caught earlier. It was injured but not dead, dragging itself around with its front legs. The cat was still in the garden but had left it alone because I was there. I went inside and watched through the window as the cat ate it."

"I thought you said you killed it," Ada said.

"I killed it because I left it on its own."

"You're right," Ada said. She was quiet for a moment. She felt angry with him. I would never have done that, she thought. "Why did you leave it?" she asked.

"I wanted to see if the cat would actually do it. I almost couldn't believe that it would."

She imagined meeting him. He would be perfect for her in every way because he was a part of her. He would understand her intuitively. He would love her in the way she had always wanted to be loved.

"But it did," she said, out loud.

"I was impressed," Darius said. "It was a type of action I have never seen in a person."

"That's why people are better than animals," Ada said.

"I don't think so," Darius said. "I think it's the opposite."

"It's good to be held back."

"What do you want to be held back from?"

"I want to always put myself first."

"I feel like that," Darius said. "I only had a girlfriend once, but if she wanted to spend time with me and I wasn't quite in the mood, I found it was impossible to compromise. I always put myself first. When she tried to force me not to, it made me panic."

"I'm the opposite," Ada said.

"Then we make a good pairing," he said.

Ada hung up the phone. She was haunted by the cat and the mouse. She tried to forget about it, but when she was trying to get to sleep that night it appeared, the determined mouse dragging itself through the grass while the cat watched from a distance, a black shadow in the sunny garden. She imagined Darius as a small, blond child. She felt angry with him for leaving. She felt angry with the cat for eating the mouse, and angry with the mouse for being so weak and yet still believing that it could survive.

SHE FITTED IN more in the facility than she ever had before. She understood that the inhabitants weren't supposed to talk to one another. They all lived parallel lives, fitting in comfortably alongside each other but never intersecting. Ada was unusual in that she talked to Don and the woman who brought her food. The others lived in their own dreamlands, drifting down the corridors with satisfied smiles on their faces, experiencing things she had no access to. Everybody saw something different, Don told her.

"How do they know what those things look like?" Ada asked. "I thought you came from somewhere else."

"Our world is very similar to yours" was all he would say.

"To me it looks kind of like a hospital," she said. For a long time, he didn't respond. Then he told her never to tell anyone else what she saw, and under no circumstances was she to ask another person to describe what they were seeing.

She experimented with changing things. One day she left her room and imagined a larger and more comfortable bed. When she reentered the room, it was there. She imagined the bathroom as twice the size, and all made of white marble, with a claw-foot bathtub. It never felt natural. After hours spent thinking of small alterations, she usually undid them the moment she'd wished them into reality. Sometimes she went out into the corridors to watch the others. It seemed so effortless for them to want things. She wanted to ask them for ideas, but remembered what Don had told her.

The morning after her conversation with Darius, she woke up when the lights came on. There was something on the floor of her room. She had changed the white carpet for wooden floorboards covered by a large rattan rug, similar to one her mother had kept in the kitchen of their house when she was growing up. In the center of the rug there was a rusty stain. She got out of bed, hoping that the stain would come out of the carpet. Looking around the room, she saw a small shadow in the corner beneath her desk. She got down on the floor to see it more clearly. It was the firm, soft body of a mouse.

She called the woman.

"There's a mouse in my room," Ada said, when she arrived at the door.

"Did you want it to be there?" the woman asked.

"No," Ada said. "It's in the corner." The woman looked under the desk. The mouse was accompanied by a smear of dried blood. She stood up again.

"Do you want me to take it away?" she asked.

"If I imagine that it's gone, will it disappear?" Ada asked.

"Did you try already?"

"Yes." Ada had closed her eyes and opened them again, imagining a clean floor and unblemished carpet, but the mouse remained.

"Then why did you ask?"

Ada didn't reply. She saw confusion flicker across the woman's face. With a slightly furrowed brow she bent down again and picked up the mouse in her hand.

"I'll get rid of it," she said. She looked at Ada. "Don't worry. It doesn't mean anything."

"How did it get in here?" Ada asked.

"It came from you," she said. "There's no other way. But we all want things sometimes without realizing we want them."

Before Ada could respond, the woman left the room with the mouse cupped in her palm.

Ada sat down on her bed. The stain on the rug had disappeared with the woman. There was no trace of it left. She decided to take a bath.

The bathroom was still made of white marble. She didn't like it, but she couldn't think of anything to replace it with. As she turned on the taps, she realized that she could imagine the bath already full. She climbed in. The water was almost too hot. It covered her to her neck.

She thought about Darius. It was hard not to imagine him as a real person, to wonder what he was doing in Poznań. She wanted to talk to him. It was so easy—she never had to explain herself. Closing her eyes, she imagined him coming into the room and sitting beside her. She would tell him about the mouse, and he would listen to her with a serious face, looking down at the tiled floor.

She opened her eyes. The room was empty. She asked herself what she had expected. There had been no indication that it was possible to bring imaginary people to life. He existed only on the other end of the phone. If she wanted to talk to somebody real, she could talk to the woman, or Don, although something about the woman's face when she saw the mouse had scared Ada. It was as if something had happened that was not meant to happen. Ada wondered if it was possible that she had willed the mouse into being without realizing what she was doing. She supposed that it made sense. The bathroom was filled with steam. On her shoulder, the place where the mole had been was smooth and unmarked.

She got out of the bath. Her skin was pink and hot. There was a thick blue bathrobe on the back of the door, and she put it on, tying the cord tightly around her waist. She went back into her bedroom and got into bed. Sliding in between the fresh sheets, she felt like she could spend the rest of her life moving between the bath and the bed, making microadjustments in her temperature. She picked up the phone and asked for a coffee, then picked it up again and changed it to a cup of tea and waffles with honey and cream.

The woman knocked on the door. When she came in Ada sat up.

"What did you do with the mouse?" she asked.

"I threw it away," the woman said. "What else would I do with it. It's not my mouse."

"Can I ask you something?" Ada said.

"Yes," the woman said.

"What am I meant to do?" Ada said.

"How should I know?" the woman said. "Enjoy your waffles."

Ada looked at the waffles. Each of the squares held a pool of butter, traversed by strings of honey. The cream had melted. She felt clean and new after her bath and the stickiness of the plate was off-putting. She wondered if she would eat and rearrange her bathroom forever. There were so many other things she could do. She thought about calling her mother but decided not to.

She thought about the mouse. If it, a living thing, had become real, there was no reason for Darius not to do the same. The mouse was dead, but the stain on the carpet indicated that it had at one point been alive: it had dragged itself into the corner. If she wanted him enough, she could make him real. It would be everything that had been missing before—somebody whose existence was tailored to loving her, somebody who could never leave.

She imagined it. Darius would knock gently on the door and when she opened it, he would give her a hug. He would be warm and gentle, a soft pillow for her to rest her head on. She imagined him coming in and saying, "I'm here, and I'm never going to leave." She wanted it more than she'd ever wanted anything.

Nothing happened. Disappointed, Ada got out of bed. She went into the corridor and wandered aimlessly past the endless blank doors. The mouse had appeared without her thinking about it, as if it had willed itself into existence. Maybe she would have to wait for Darius to do the same thing. She walked towards the swimming pool. Maybe she would ask Don to help her. When she reached the swimming pool, she took off her bathrobe and got into the water. After swimming, she thought, she could have another bath and wash her hair, and then get back into bed. In the pool, instead of swimming lengths, she floated on her back. There was no need for exercise in the facility.

As she floated, she imagined that she was in a jungle, surrounded by animals of all kinds. She could hear the birds calling to each other, smell the rich earth and rotting fruit that burst open on the ground. Colorful flowers made a canopy around her as she floated down a slow-moving river. A butterfly landed for a moment on her arm before fluttering away. A tiger slept on the riverbank in a patch of sun. A snake dragged itself silently through the undergrowth. Ada could feel warm mist on her face, and when she reached down, she felt thick, wet mud beneath her fingers.

Then the scene changed. It was her mother's kitchen. She was looking into the brightly colored fish tank her mother had bought her, except she couldn't find any of the fish. She thought they must be hiding behind the plastic rocks. It was only when she examined the pebble-covered floor that she saw that the fish had eaten each other. Her mother, disturbed, poured the tank out over the lawn, and left the half-chewed bodies to rot.

Confused, Ada opened her eyes. It was the first time something from her past had breached the walls of the facility. Before she could think further, she was distracted by the sight of a man standing on the far side of the room. Although Ada had never seen him before, she knew that it was Darius. The first thing that surprised her was that he wasn't how she'd imagined him. His brown hair was thinning at the temples. His body was long and taut, like a bow, and his shoulders were slightly hunched.

They were in her room. He sat on the chair beside her desk. Ada was cross-legged on the bed with the blanket over her knees. She couldn't think of anything to say to him.

"Where did you come from?" she asked him, eventually.

"I was in Poznań. I was walking along the river. The sky was very gray. I thought that I should come here and be with you."

"You wanted to come here?"

"Of course," he said.

Ada looked at him. The fine bones of his face reminded her of fluted porcelain. His eyes were brown. He wore jeans and a knitted sweater of olive-green wool.

"Are you real?" she said.

"I don't know," he said.

"Do you want something to eat?" she asked.

"I'm not very hungry," he said. "I can't remember eating before." He stretched his legs out under the desk. "This is a nice room."

"I wanted to change it," Ada said, "but I couldn't think of how anything could be different."

Darius came to sit beside her on the bed. He had taken off his shoes, and she saw that his socks were blue, slightly darker than her trousers.

"We can do anything you want," he said.

"Let's go for a walk," she said.

TOGETHER THEY WENT into the corridor. Ada had changed into a blue dress. It was the first time she had worn a dress in years. They passed the swimming pool and thought about going in, but Ada decided that she didn't want to. Darius held her hand. It felt strange to be in his company, after talking for so long on the phone. Their conversation was stilted. Darius didn't seem to notice. He looked closely at everything they passed, examining the doors and light sockets, tracing a finger along the banister when they climbed the stairs. After a while Ada asked him what he was looking for.

"All of this is you," he said. "So all of it is important."

Eventually they reached a door. Ada stopped in front of it.

"Let's go in here," she said.

Darius turned the handle and pushed it open. Ada followed him in. It was the jungle she had imagined in the swimming pool. He closed the door behind them. Trees stretched themselves far above her head like the ceiling of a church. Some of the deep-green leaves were as large as her body, or larger. It was warm and wet. There were huge purple and yellow flowers hanging from the vines that wrapped themselves around the slender tree trunks. They smelled sweet and faintly sick.

The stamens were like trumpets covered in fine red pollen. She turned to Darius.

"I thought about this earlier," she said. "I imagined it."

They went farther in. The river was there, broad and leisurely. The water was brown, full of sediment. On the bank lay the sleeping tiger. Ada wondered if it could hurt them. It belongs to me, she thought. It couldn't hurt her, or it would be hurting itself. The air was warmer than it had been in the corridor. Beneath her feet the ground was damp. Insects buzzed around her head. She followed Darius towards the river. Alongside the water there was a bank of bright green grass. Ada sat down in it.

"I don't think they have grass like this in real jungles," Darius said.

"I've never been in a jungle," Ada said.

She wanted to go swimming. She took off her top and trousers and folded them neatly on the riverbank. Darius didn't look at her. In her blue underwear she waded into the water. The riverbed was sandy, rather than muddy, and her feet stirred up eddies of silt. Brown leaves floated on the surface. At the deepest point the water came up to her thighs. She sat down so that it flowed around her shoulders. Darius sat on the bank, in the shade of a fern with broad, spiked leaves.

"Are you coming in?" she asked.

"No," he said. "I'm afraid of the water."

"Why? There's nothing in here."

"You don't know that."

The tiger was directly in front of Ada. She could see the orange-and-black pattern of its thick fur. In the sun it seemed to glow. Up close, it was bigger than she had thought, and denser, as if it were made of gold, or filled with sand. It opened its black eyes and looked at her. A shiver went through her. She stayed where she was, in the center of the river. There was no way it would attack her. If it did, she would have no chance. It stood up, shook the dirt and broken sticks from its coat, and disappeared into the trees.

"See?" she called to Darius. He didn't respond. He had taken off his sweater and was lying with his head in the shade and his body in the sun. Ada thought he looked peaceful.

She looked around. In both directions there was a curve in the river that she couldn't see beyond. Above her head, the trees obscured the sky. What she could see was white instead of blue. If she walked into the forest, would she eventually meet the far wall of the room? She imagined that where she ran out of jungle to invent, it would begin to repeat itself, and so could go on forever.

Standing up, she waded through the water towards the bend in the river. Although it appeared nearby, it didn't seem to get any closer. She climbed out of the water and walked along the soft grass bank. It seemed to curve endlessly without revealing anything new. She kept going, fighting her way through the vine-laden trees that hung over the water. Eventually she crouched under the fronds of a large fern and saw Darius sitting on the grass.

He jumped up when he saw her.

"I couldn't see where you'd gone," he said. "I was scared."

"I wanted to see what was up the river," she said. He didn't reply. His thin face was pale. She put her clothes on over her wet underwear. They went back towards the door. Darius was cheerful again by the time they reached it.

"That was beautiful," he said. "You think of such beautiful things."

"I thought of you," she said. He smiled. They walked back to the room together in silence.

THEY WERE SITTING on the bed. A bath was running and steam drifted through the open door.

"Tell me more about Poznań," Ada said.

"I don't have very much to tell you," Darius said. "I already told you about my father and walking along the river, and the cat and the mouse."

"Do you know everything that I know?"

"I knew where I was when I arrived here. I don't know what you're thinking, but I feel like I know you very well."

She wanted to ask him if he had his own thoughts but didn't know how to phrase it. It seemed like there was no way he could say no, even if it was the truth.

"Are you happy to be here?" she asked.

"Yes," he said. "Very happy."

Ada listened to the bath running. Suddenly she didn't want to be immersed in water again. She went into the bathroom and turned the taps off. She was tired.

"I'm going to sleep," she said to Darius.

"Do you want me to sleep with you?" he asked her.

"Only if you want to," she said.

"I want to make you happy," he said.

"But are you tired?"

"No."

"Then I don't want you to sleep with me."

He took her hand.

"Can't I want to do something because it's what you want?" he asked her.

"It's not real if it's only because I want it," Ada said. "I want you to want to do it on your own."

"I don't know how to do that," Darius said. "I'm not real."

"Neither am I," Ada said.

Darius fell asleep quickly. Ada got out of bed quietly, not wanting to wake him. Her tiredness was gone. The lights dimmed for the arrival of the imitative night. In her room they went out, but in the corridor it was never completely dark.

She wanted to find the jungle again. She tried to retrace their steps, but all the corridors looked the same. At night it reminded her of a cruise ship. Her bare feet were silent on the carpeted floor. After a few minutes, she chose a door and stopped in front of it. When she touched the door handle, it was cold. She pushed it open. It was the same jungle. The night sky gave a dim light, but all she could see were the shadows of the trees. She heard a rustling but didn't feel scared. Things were alive all around her.

She took a few steps forwards. She only wanted to see it, then she would go back and get into bed. She put her foot down and felt something round and soft. It was too dark to make out what it was, so she bent down and picked it up. In the moonlight she saw the body of a dead mouse, its hind legs chewed away by some kind of animal. She dropped it in horror. Blood stained her fingers. As she turned to go, something in the undergrowth caught her eye. It was the tiger, black eyes staring out at her, the solid outline of its body perfectly still, as if it were waiting for a chance to strike.

She left the room.

When she got back to her bedroom Darius was awake. He asked her where she'd gone.

"I went to walk around," she said. "I couldn't sleep."

He held out an arm for her and she got into bed.

"I had a terrible dream," he said. "I dreamt that I looked down at my body and it turned into a mass of snakes. One by one they slithered away until there was nothing left. Then I woke up and you weren't here. I was scared."

"I'm sorry," Ada said. Nobody apart from her mother had ever needed her before. Surprised, she found it made her feel nothing. It was him that she wanted to need. "I'm here now," she said.

He hugged her tightly. In the dark, his body was like a warm cave that she could crawl into. I have everything I want, she thought.

ADA SPENT A lot of time watching him. She wanted to see if he reminded her of herself. After a while, she realized that she wouldn't know what to look for. She had heard once that if you saw yourself walking down the street, you would see a stranger. To an observer, the similarities between Darius and herself might be obvious, but for her they were impossible to see.

There was something about him that reminded her of a child. If she went somewhere without him, he would be tense and nervous when she returned. Sometimes he looked at her with wide, fearful eyes, as if he was afraid that she might hurt him. When she asked him what was wrong, he said, "I'm afraid if you're gone for too long, I'll disappear." Occasionally he suggested that they go back to the room with the jungle, but Ada didn't want to. She didn't tell Darius about the mouse. She just said that they'd already been there.

It disturbed her that he knew where he came from. They were on a beach, pebbled rather than sandy, stretched out together on a towel next to an ocean that was more gray than blue. Behind them was a thick line of dark forest. Ada could smell pine trees on the breeze, mixed together with salt from the ocean. The sky was overcast and it was cold. The shoreline was decorated with bleached driftwood and the tangled remnants of fishing nets. They had found it in a room down a wide corridor, far away from Ada's bedroom.

"But you exist without me," Ada said. "You don't evaporate when I leave the room."

"I know," Darius said. "It's just a feeling."

"Do you remember things from your life?" Ada asked him.

"Not really. I mostly think about you."

"What do you think about me?"

"I wonder what it's like to be you."

Ada shaded her eyes with her hand. Beside her, Darius's body was pale and thin. She wanted to inflate it until it was solid and round, capable of standing up on its own.

"What do you think it's like to be me?" she asked.

"I think it's scary," he said. "Is that right?"

"I don't know," Ada said. "I don't feel scared."

"I do," Darius said. "I feel scared when you go swimming because I don't know what would happen to me if you drowned."

"I can't drown," Ada said.

"You don't know that," he said. "We're sitting here, talking to each other. You can't say it's not real. When somebody dies in a dream it feels just as bad."

Ada stood up and went towards the water. Darius stayed on the towel. It was cold around her ankles, and the pebbles were unsteady beneath her feet. Her skin prickled and goose bumps rose along her arms. She waded in until it was up to her waist and looked at the horizon, appearing and disappearing behind the shallow waves. She knew that Darius was watching her. Despite the cold, she waded in deeper, and started to swim. He would be worried about her drowning. She wanted him to worry, to be scared that she would leave him. Something about his weakness made her want to punish him.

She swam for a long time. Eventually when she turned around to look at the shore, everything she saw began merging into a line of green and a line of gray. Her feet and hands had begun to go numb. She didn't feel tired. Absentmindedly, she considered letting herself sink. Darius would think she had drowned. She imagined his distress. He wouldn't stop existing because she would still be alive, under the water, out of sight, but he would believe that she was gone.

She started to swim back. It would be like abandoning a child. Ada pictured the hyacinth-blue walls of her bedroom in her mother's house. She remembered going downstairs after her father left, looking for somebody to take care of her, and finding that everybody was gone. The kitchen was dark. There was no food in the fridge. In a cupboard, she found her father's protein supplements. She sat on the sofa in the living room and tried to block out the sound of her own blood pumping in her ears. Late in the evening, her mother came back. Her thin body barely cast a shadow on the wall.

Beneath the water, she imagined thin, pale hands reaching up towards her, fingers as large as the masts of sunken ships. There was no reason that Darius should have to be alone because he loved her. Her feet touched the ground. She rose, dripping, from the water and made her way back up the stony incline. As she climbed the bank, she thought she saw something moving behind the tree line; a white-and-orange flash between the dark spires of the pine trees. She looked for a moment more but saw nothing. There was a cold breeze that raised the hair on her arms. When she finally reached Darius, she saw that he was crying. He cried inconsolably. It made no difference when she crouched down beside him and wrapped her cold, wet arms around his neck.

"I'm sorry," she said. "I came back."

He tried to say something through his tears but couldn't get the words out. Ada stood up and he steadied himself with her arm. Together they went back to the room. He sat bent over on her bed, shaking so hard that Ada was worried that he would break up into pieces. He only stopped crying when he fell asleep, his head resting on her lap.

She stayed awake all night, watching Darius sleep. If she loved him enough, she thought, that love would eventually find its way through him and back to her. When she was sure he wouldn't wake up, she crept out into the corridor, as she'd done the night she found the mouse in the jungle, and sat outside the door cross-legged, like a watchman. Just before the lights came on, she went back to bed.

When he woke up, his eyes were red and swollen.

"I don't know what's happening to me," he said.

"It'll be okay," Ada said. "I'm not going to leave you."

He looked up at her. With his unkempt hair he looked ragged and distressed. Beneath the bedsheets he was still wearing the clothes he'd arrived in.

"This isn't how I thought it would be," he said. "I thought you needed love, and I would give it to you. Now it feels like I'm desperate, and you want to escape."

"I don't want to escape," Ada said. "This is all I've ever wanted." So why, she thought, aren't I happy? Darius looked away. She took his bony hand and held it tightly.

THE NEXT DAY they wandered the corridors, looking for a room. Ada had said to Darius that if she could find a room with her parents in it, she could solve the problem.

"I just need to talk to them," she said. "I need to apologize for leaving. After that, you can make me happy."

Looking at the doors, she felt nervous. They made her feel sick, as if the floor was moving underneath her feet. Darius was quiet and pale.

After a while they found it. When Ada touched the handle, it seemed to call to her. When she opened it, she felt like the bottom of her stomach had fallen away. Darius was just behind her but as soon as she entered the room the door closed behind her, locking him out.

Around a table sat a family, but they weren't Ada's family. They were perfectly still, but their bodies had the soft warmth of living skin. They were dressed in clothes that reminded Ada of her grandparents. The mother wore a dress with a stiff collar and a long skirt that stuck out around her in a circle. Her waist was thick, and her hair tightly curled. She was standing up and leaning over the table to light a candle. Around her neck was a string of pearls. To her left was the father, in a brown suit. He was young and handsome, with a square jaw and a thick brush of hair. The two children looked almost the same age. They sat leaning in towards each other like two magnets. The room was dark, lit by a lamp in the corner, but the scene seemed to emit a bright, warm glow. Ada noticed that there was an empty chair at the table, between the children and their mother. She sat down in it. Ada was so sure they were alive that she could almost feel their breath on her skin, but they didn't move. She wondered who they were.

"Let me in," she said, but nothing happened. They were pretending to be dead. Frustrated, she reached out to touch the mother's arm. The mother jerked away from her, and Ada jumped.

"What do you think you're doing?" the mother said.

"Sorry," Ada said. "I wanted to see if you were alive."

"Your behavior is disgraceful," the mother said.

"I want to be part of your family," Ada said.

"Well, you can't," the mother said. "You're not like us. We're good."

The others started to come to life. The father reached for a dish in the center of the table and speared a slice of ham with his fork. The children talked in whispers. None of them seemed to notice Ada. When she tried to meet their gaze, they avoided looking at her.

"Please," Ada said. The mother stared at her with black eyes. Ada felt something in her chest. It was like a hard ball wedged behind her sternum.

"Go to your room," the mother said. "You're not welcome."

Ada stood up. She felt tears on her face. Behind the table there was a dark corridor. She went down it and found the farthest room. Inside was a single bed, the frame made of intricate wrought iron, covered in a floral bedspread that was cold to the touch. On the wall was a painting of a landscape in winter, a barren tree covered in snow. She sat on the edge of the bed and the mattress sagged beneath her. In the corner was an enamel washbasin with a mirror above it.

"I'm sorry," she said, out loud, to nobody. Standing up, she went over to the mirror. When she looked at it, she saw that she had no reflection.

She found Darius waiting for her in the corridor.

"You don't love me," she said to him. She stated it simply, as a fact.

"Yes, I do," he said. "What do you mean?"

"I don't believe you," she said.

Darius tried to hug her, but she pushed him away.

"Leave me alone," she said. She opened another door and slammed it behind her. The room was a blank gray box, as if it hadn't had time to become something else. She sat against the wall and pulled her knees up against her chest. Eventually she lay down on the hard ground and tried to fall asleep, but when she closed her eyes, she remembered the promise she'd made never to abandon Darius. She got up and tried to open the door, but it was locked. Panic flooded her as she tugged at it. "Darius," she called. "I can't get out." There was no sound from the other side.

She sat back down. The gray walls seemed to tighten. For a moment she was afraid that she would be crushed. The room was like a prison cell. She imagined Darius on the other side of the door, distraught. Part of her was relieved to be shielded from his distress, but a stronger part wanted to find him and make him believe that everything was okay. Tears came to her eyes. Of course he loved her. Why couldn't she see it when she was with him? Suddenly she felt overwhelmingly tired. She let her head sink down to the concrete floor and thought briefly about bashing her brains out.

EVENTUALLY THE DOOR opened. Ada wasn't sure how long she'd been stuck. She'd fallen asleep on the hard floor and had dreamt of nothing. Sleep had calmed her down. She guessed that was why the door had opened. Her cheek and head hurt. It was the soft click of the lock that had woken her up.

Darius wasn't in the corridor. Ada guessed that he'd gone back to her room, but she was surprised. She had expected to find him asleep in the corridor. It was night and the lights were dim. She went quietly down the hallway, disoriented and afraid of what she would find when she reached her bedroom. Absently she wondered if it was possible for Darius to kill himself, and what would happen to her if he did. Even if he wanted to, there wasn't really any way for him to do it.

She turned a corner. The facility was like a giant brain, especially at night, when the soft light lent it an organic feeling, as if it were growing and changing around her. There was a person standing at the end of the corridor, their back turned to her. They hadn't heard her coming. Ada stopped. It wasn't somebody she'd seen before. They were standing in front of an open door. Whatever was in the room cast a wedge of yellow light onto the carpet outside.

Slowly Ada approached. As she got closer, she saw that the person was a woman with short brown hair. She didn't turn around until Ada was right behind her.

"What're you doing?" the woman asked.

"I'm trying to find my way back to my room."

"Are you lost?"

"No."

The woman looked at Ada. She had freckles on her cheeks and a pointed nose. Her short hair was tucked behind her ears. She was standing in the doorway of the room. Over her shoulder, Ada could see what looked like a huge screen, or a window.

"I know who you are," the woman said.

"Who am I?"

The woman laughed a high, tinkling laugh. It sounded like a handful of teaspoons being dropped down the stairs. Ada wondered why she was laughing.

"Do you want to see something?"

"Yes."

The woman stepped back from the doorway so that Ada could see into the room. Ada moved forwards, into the light. The room was small, but the screen took up almost an entire wall. It showed the skyline of a gray, overcast city. Something like a thick white rib cage stuck up from the skyline.

"This is Australia." She paused. "It was meant to be sunny." She paused again. There was something strange about her demeanor. She was unlike the other people in the facility whom Ada had met. Her brown eyes, set in a spray of delicate wrinkles, were sensible and human. She reminded Ada of a teacher. "Where do you want to go?"

"London," Ada said. The woman had something in her hand. It looked like a matte black ball, but when she moved it, the image on the screen moved in and out.

"I know what you want to see," the woman said. She rolled the ball between her palms and the picture went so far out that Ada could see the shapes of the continents. The ocean was a deeper blue than she had expected. Then it moved in again. Ada saw London, bisected by the Thames. It was night and the sky was dark, full of stars, and the streets were lit by an orange glow. It took a moment for Ada to realize they were looking at her apartment block. "Look," the woman said. "Look in the window."

There were only lights on in a few of the apartments. In one of the windows Ada could see the outline of a person.

"Do you know what that is?" the woman asked.

"No."

"That's you."

Ada looked at the black shape. It didn't move. She recognized the faint yellow light of her bedroom lamp.

"You're not meant to tell me what you can see," Ada said.

"It's on a screen," the woman said. "It's not private." Ada turned to look at her. The woman put the ball in her pocket and smoothed the front of the neat white shirt she was wearing. "You shouldn't be scared of it," she said.

"I'm not." It sat perfectly still, framed by the window, facing away from them. Ada couldn't believe how alone it was, sitting by the window in the middle of the night. Then, abruptly, it got up and closed the blinds. Ada kept staring at the blank facade of the building. "Where do you make them?" she asked the woman.

"We don't make them," the woman said. "They're grown."

"Where?"

"Not here." She took the ball back out of her pocket. It was smooth. "I can't explain it. You wouldn't understand."

"I want to know what I am."

"It doesn't matter," the woman said. "It won't help." She was moving the ball so that the picture on the screen changed slowly, morphing into the soft green countryside that Ada recognized as just outside of London. "You all think that will help, but it doesn't." The picture moved restlessly through muddy woodland and open fields filled with broken stalks of wheat. It reminded Ada of where her grandparents had lived. She felt homesick for the cold air. In the winter there would be frost on the spiderwebs. "What helps is what you surround yourself with. You have to know what you want to look at."

"I don't understand."

"I know," the woman said. "You should go back to your room." The screen went black. Ada stepped back into the dim corridor. The woman followed her, closing the door behind them. "It was nice to meet you," she said. "Don't tell Don I showed you that."

"I won't," Ada said. The woman walked briskly away in the direction that Ada had come. Her shirt rustled audibly in the quiet of the corridor. Ada turned to watch her go, and noticed that her small, bony feet were bare.

SHE FOUND DARIUS sleeping in her room and shook him until his eyes opened. They were red and swollen.

"I saw something," she said. "I saw myself." He looked up at her.

"What are you talking about?"

"My replacement." He looked away from her, down at where his hands lay on the bedspread. She was sitting over him, her hand on his narrow shoulder.

"I don't know what you mean."

"I didn't mean to leave you," she said. "I came back as soon as I could." He didn't respond. His face was pressed into the pillow, as if he was trying not to hear or see her. "It was what was in the room," she said. "Do you want to know about it?"

"You can tell me," he said, without turning his face to her.

"It was a family," Ada said. "And they wouldn't let me in. Then I realized that nobody loved me, and nobody ever could love me, and I didn't love anybody either."

"But I'm here," Darius said. "And I love you."

"I know," Ada said. "I'm sorry." She was frustrated. She had given him the answer, and she wanted him to sit up and say that everything was okay. "What's wrong?"

"I don't know," he said. "You being back doesn't make it better." He paused. Ada lay down and put her arms around him. His body was cold. The door that had closed between them would not reopen.

"I'm going to kill the tiger," she said. The thought came to her impulsively. He didn't reply. She got up again and went to the wardrobe. He watched her pensively as she got dressed. The thought of a mission energized her. Staying in the room with Darius was impossible. It occurred to her that even in wanting to save him she was trying to get away from him, but she pushed the thought away. Standing in front of the mirror she thought of a suit of armor. It materialized around her. In the mirror she saw a warrior. She imagined herself a sword with a long, sharp blade. It was heavy in her hand, and the metal was cold.

"You look like Joan of Arc," Darius said.

She went out into the corridor. She wasn't sure what she was going to do, only that she had to do something to bring her and Darius back together. The tiger seemed like a sensible target. It would be waiting for her in the jungle, crouched in the undergrowth and staring out from its deep, black eyes. She wondered what would happen when she killed it. Suddenly she felt upset, as if she didn't know what she was doing. Everything seemed to spin around her as she walked down the corridor. The armor was heavy on her body, and it was hard to keep the blade of the sword from snagging on the carpet.

She was sure that she had seen the tiger on the beach. It was following her like a bad omen. She was scared of it. She hated the way it looked at her with its eyes like two wet stones, like it wanted to eat her. On the way to the room with the jungle she found Don. He was walking in the other direction.

"Ada," he said. "Where are you going?"

"Nowhere," she said. He smiled. Ada looked at his face. For a moment she wanted to tell him what the woman with the short hair had shown her. His eyes were surrounded by thousands of tiny wrinkles, but his skin kept its structure rather than sagging off his jaw. His eyes were pale blue. She remembered the smooth tips of his fingers. Now his hands were hidden in his pockets. If you could build yourself a body, why choose to be forgettable? He'd said that it was only the inside that mattered. The outside was a mask. Through her armor, Ada smiled back. "I'm going to kill a tiger," she said.

"Good luck," he said. He passed her by and continued on down the corridor.

The room with the jungle found her before she could find it. The sounds of birds calling drifted to her down the carpeted hallway. Stopping in front of the door, she imagined that it was looking at her, challenging her. She twisted the handle and pushed it open. It wasn't immediately obvious what was different. Warm mist enveloped her, and beneath her clothes she began to sweat. The trees still waved their branches overhead, and she could hear the river running. It was only when she looked down at the ground that she saw it was littered with the bodies of dead animals. There were birds and mice, snakes, furred mammals that Ada didn't recognize, even a monkey, curled up as if it was sleeping. All of them were mangled and twisted, feathers and fur stained with blood. There was a rancid smell in the air. The birdsong had fallen away into silence. When Ada looked up, nothing moved in the trees.

The armor was too heavy and her body began to ache. The sword was heavy in her hands. Sweat poured off her forehead. She knew that if she kept going inwards, she would find the tiger eventually, or it would find her. There was nowhere to hide in the room. It wasn't a real jungle; there was only so far that either of them could go.

She thought about Darius, curled up in her bed. He was in pain. Although she had made him, he needed her more than she needed him. She wished that he would be independent, so that he could come and go as he wanted. His love didn't feel like love. It was too clinging. He had no other choice but to love her. His existence depended on it. She reached the river and splashed her way through it. On the other side things felt different. The sky was darker and some of the heat was gone from the air. Ada cut her way through the undergrowth, pushing aside the small, destroyed bodies beneath her feet.

Then she found it. Breaking through a dense wall of trees, she came across a bank of rock. In one jagged corner was a narrow opening, the entrance of which was stained the color of rust. Ada knew the tiger was inside. She hit her sword against the rock, raising a white mark on the gray surface. A noise came from within the cave, and the tiger appeared. It was smaller than she remembered, but the smallness lent it a viciousness that scared her even more. When it saw Ada, it made a rumbling that was like nothing she'd ever heard before. She felt fear deep in her stomach, so deep that it felt like being turned inside out. She raised her sword as the tiger flattened its ears and crouched. It didn't matter, she told herself. None of it was real.

It was over quickly. The tiger leapt towards her, and the sword went into its mouth and came out the other side. Ada held on to the hilt as the heavy body sagged and then fell to the ground. It caught her with an outstretched paw on the side of her face. She felt blood running down her cheek. It didn't hurt. Sitting down beside the body, she closed her eyes. The armor lifted itself off her. Her hands shook. Her mind was still and empty. The body of the tiger was warm. She leaned against it. She thought that she should get back to Darius, to tell him about her victory, but when she opened her eyes, she saw that what she had been leaning against wasn't the body of the tiger, but the body of a man. When she looked closer, she saw that it was Atticus, pale in a pool of his own blood, the sword embedded in his chest. His eyes were closed. She stood up. As she turned to go, she saw something move, and a whisper of orange and white disappeared through the trees.

———

DARIUS WAS WAITING for her.

"Did you kill it?" he asked.

"Yes," she said. She didn't tell him that it had been Atticus. She had left the body on the jungle floor, to be eaten by birds and insects. The tiger meant nothing. It wasn't an impostor; it was a shadow puppet, another projection. Atticus was a part of her, a part that would never go away.

"What will happen now?" he asked.

"I was hoping it would change things," she said. "I thought the tiger was making you scared."

"I think I feel different," he said. "I don't know."

"I can't really change anything," Ada said.

"What do you mean?" he said.

"I could imagine whatever I wanted, and it would still all be inside me, so nothing will ever be different."

"What're you going to do?" Darius asked.

Ada touched her cheek. The blood had dried. Going into the bathroom, she turned on the taps of the bath. In the mirror she saw a disheveled, frightened person who she didn't recognize. She went back to the bedroom.

"I don't know," she said. "I guess we'll have to stay like this forever."

"I'll get better," Darius said. "It just might take time. I want to be what you imagined."

Ada took his hand.

"You won't get better," she said. "Everything I make has something wrong with it, because there's something wrong with me." Too late, she realized the purpose of the fake body.

"Things aren't that bad," he said. "We have adventures. We look after each other."

Ada looked at him. The Polish accent he had arrived with was gone. Now he sounded like her. While she was gone, he had replaced his jumper and jeans with a blue T-shirt and trousers from her cupboard. He was so thin that they fit him perfectly. She tried to remember what she had imagined him as before he arrived; the real estate agent from Poznań walking down a windy street in his anorak, on his way to watch television with his old father.

"I can't feel it," she said.

He seemed to realize before she did. A tear ran down his cheek.

"It's happening," he said.

"I'm sorry," she said. "I don't love you enough."

He put his head on her lap. Ada ran her fingers through his thin hair. He had a small mole behind his ear, barely visible. Reaching up to touch her scalp, Ada felt a raised bump in the same place. She held his hands as tightly as she could, as if she was trying to capture whatever was draining out of them, until there was nothing left to clutch at but blue cotton bedsheets. In the bathroom, hot water overflowed onto the floor. After a while, she got up and turned off the taps.

TIME PASSED. ADA wasn't sure how much of it. It was easier to let the days take on a circular structure, where the same day happened over and over again, rotating around her. She stopped planning things and just allowed them to happen. Like she had with Darius, she wandered in and out of rooms, not imagining, but waiting. The other people who drifted down the corridors didn't speak to her, but Ada understood that the fabric of the facility was made up of all of them, not just her. The woman continued to deliver her meals, and sometimes she saw Don from a distance, flitting between rooms like a ghost.

Although she didn't want to be on her own, it had happened. She couldn't think of anybody else to invent. Darius had been her best attempt.

After a week, she began to feel nebulous, like she was floating through space. She had started sleeping with the low lamp on so there was no real difference between day and night. Often, she slept for twelve hours or more. Once she started sleeping later, she started staying up late into the night, so she could creep around the corridors while everything was dark and silent.

HUNGRY FOR COMPANY, she went to find a room with someone to talk to. She wanted to find the short-haired woman, but instead she found a girl with long black hair. There was an empty chair beside her. She looked up when Ada came in.

"Hello," she said.

"Hello," Ada said. She sat down in the empty chair, so that she and the girl were next to each other, like in a waiting room.

"What's up?" the girl asked. She wore bracelets on her slim wrists and a gold cross around her neck. On her feet were a pair of sandals with straps of braided leather.

"I broke up with my boyfriend," Ada said.

"Oh," the girl said. "I'm sorry."

"It's okay," Ada said. "We weren't right for each other. We were trying to give each other the wrong things."

"I know what that's like," the girl said. "I had a boyfriend who kept telling me that he wanted to give me space when it was the last thing I wanted. Really it was him who wanted space. He couldn't tell the difference between me and himself."

"My boyfriend got upset if I wanted space," Ada said.

"Maybe he felt like you were abandoning him," the girl said. "Some people are very sensitive about that."

"I was abandoning him."

"They can always tell," the girl said. "Always."

Ada looked around the room. There was a low table with a lamp, and a picture of a frozen ocean on the wall.

"Where are we?" she asked.

"I'm here for the doctor," the girl said. "I think I might be pregnant."

"Will you keep it?"

"I don't want to," she said. "But I don't know if I have any choice."

There was a carpet on the floor. It was orange. Near Ada's foot was a small hole where the wooden floor showed through.

Ada looked at the painting. It was small in a large gilt frame and showed an arctic scene of icebergs and flat gray sea. In the distant background, the blank wall of a glacier rose up from the water.

She left the room. The woman would be in the facility somewhere. If she could find her, Ada thought, she could see herself again on the screen, the strange black shape that shared her outline. It scared her to think about it, but beneath the fear there was a thrill, a need to know more.

The corridor was unusually bright. Ada wondered if something was happening. Her mouth was dry. She took a right-hand turn, and then another one. There was no direction she particularly wanted to go, but she wanted to get away from her room, which had begun to feel like a cell. There was a wide flight of stairs ahead of her, and Ada took them two steps at a time. The exertion caused her heart to beat hard. She took another right turn and entered a narrow corridor that she thought she recognized. At the end was a steel door. She knew what it concealed. It was the room Don had shown her, with the watery oblong hanging in the empty space. When she reached the end of the corridor, she opened the door.

Looking carefully into the enormous mass of weightless, shifting liquid, she tried to find herself, but she could only make out individual limbs that did not appear to belong to her. Through the shape, she saw the other door. There was somebody standing on the platform in front of it, but Ada couldn't make out who it was. When they raised their hand to wave, Ada realized it was the short-haired woman. She tried shouting but the sound was lost in the vastness of the space. She imagined a bridge across the void but nothing appeared. The short-haired woman turned and disappeared through the door.

Back out in the corridor, Ada turned to the left. She would walk around the central room until she found the short-haired woman. The wall had a gentle curve, almost imperceptible, and she began to follow it. A man walked past, coming from the other direction, and smiled at her. Ada smiled back. She thought of asking him for directions but didn't. She continued on, trying to follow the curve of the wall. Soon she lost all sense of direction. When she came to a junction, she always took the right-hand turn. As a child she'd been told the way to reach the center of a maze was to keep your hand on the right-hand wall.

It seemed to her that as she got farther away from her room, the light began to change. There was no difference that she could perceive in the overhead light bulbs, but things took on a pinkish hue, then a very light green, as if she were underwater. The fabric of the carpet also seemed to shift, as if the texture of the thread was thickening and diminishing, but when Ada looked down, it always looked the same. It was just what she could feel beneath her feet.

She wondered what the short-haired woman would give her. During her stay in the facility, she had grown better at wanting things, but it still wasn't enough to make her truly happy. What she wanted was something that would give her the answer, although she was aware that she didn't really have a question. The question was made up of everything that had happened before the facility, everything that had opened up the holes in her character for which she did not have the tools to repair herself.

She was lost. Continuing on, bearing to the right, she walked until her feet and legs began to hurt. She had never been truly lost in the facility before. She wasn't scared, but she felt taken over by a determined misery, as if she had committed herself to something that she knew had no end.

Eventually she wanted to stop and go to sleep. She opened a door, imagining a bedroom, and found a room full of screens. On the screens, a video was playing on a loop. It was Darius, melting away into the bed. Ada left the room and closed the door. The lights dimmed, signifying the arrival of the night. She lay down where she was in the corridor with her back against the wall. The carpet softened itself beneath her.

When she woke up, she was disoriented. The lights were still dim. She started to walk again, past what felt like hundreds of different turns and doors. After the room with the screens, she was scared to go into any of them. Why would the facility have shown her something she didn't want to see? She felt guilty about Darius. She had made him and demolished him with the sadism of a child. It seemed like a horrific thing to do. It was easy to comfort herself with the thought that he wasn't real, that he didn't have his own thoughts and feelings, but she knew that it wasn't true. He had lived so briefly and experienced so much horror, and it was her fault.

"I'm sorry," she whispered, out loud. It made it worse to know he would forgive her, because he understood her, but she didn't understand him.

The corridor took her down a set of stairs and then up again. Ada couldn't tell which direction she was walking. She had taken every right turn—she wondered if she had made a full loop and was going back the way she came. There was no sign of the short-haired woman.

She reached a dead end. She stopped in front of it. In the half-dark, she thought she heard someone behind her and turned around, but the corridor was empty. She turned back. The wall before her was smooth and white. Set into it was a door. It was unlike the other doors in the facility, all of which were the flimsy sheets of laminated plywood found in cheap hotels. It looked heavy, and old, with a rusted metal knocker. Ada touched it, wondering what part of her it had come from. The dark wood was scarred and pitted, as if many people had tried and failed to open it. The facility had led her to what she had been looking for.

It opened easily. Ada went in.

SHE WAS STANDING on the edge of a snowy mountain. It was dark, and very cold. Ada was wearing a thick fleece and waterproof trousers. To her left, in a space where the ground leveled out, there was a large canvas tent, the sides rolled up so as to be open to the elements. Electric lamps hung in all four corners. In the middle of the tent, there was an open fire burning in a pit ringed with large stones. Trestle tables stood in a circle around it, at which an array of people was seated, all dressed in cold-weather gear. Everybody was young. Some had partially undressed, stripping down to thermal underlayers, and the floor was scattered with abandoned gloves and goggles. Outside the tent, skis were stuck upright in the snow. Ada walked farther inside. Although it was bitterly cold, the glow of firelight on the canvas roof made her feel warm.

Amongst the seated people was a man with a guitar. When Ada looked at him, he appeared to have Darius's face, but when she turned away and looked back he was a stranger. He played and sang, and the other people listened. Every time he finished a song, he would ask the crowd what they wanted next. He had a French accent. No matter what song was requested, he knew how to play it from start to finish. Ada listened as the songs they requested grew more obscure, and it seemed impossible that he would know them all by heart, but he did.

A young couple requested a song. They got up to dance in the space by the fire while the man played it. They were clumsy in their ski boots and held on to each other for balance.

There was a space at one of the tables and Ada sat down. A woman was sitting next to her.

"Where are we?" Ada asked.

"Oberlech," the woman said. She sounded German. "How do you not know?"

"I forgot," Ada said.

"Last night there was an avalanche," the woman said. She had bright red hair done in two thick braids. "A man died."

"Who was he?"

"Masha. A guide. He went out on the mountain although he knew that it was dangerous. This late in the year, the snow is not stable. They are still digging for his body." The woman turned back to the music. A colorful balaclava was tucked around her neck. The song ended, and the dancing couple returned to their seats.

Ada stood up. As she stood, she caught the eye of the dancing woman. It was her mother. Her face was tanned and she was laughing. Ada knew that the man she had danced with, who now sat closely beside her, was her father.

Ada turned away and stumbled back through the thick snow. Some distance away there was a line of dark pine trees, outlined by the snow that sat heavy on their branches. In the moonlight, it was as if they were glowing. The snow came up to her knees. She fought her way through it. As she approached the first tree her foot hit something solid. She tried to step over it but found it was too large to easily traverse. Reaching down, she pushed the snow away. The face of a young man, nearly a child, stared up at her. It was purple and twisted. For a moment it looked familiar. His ski goggles had been pushed down around his neck, and his eyes were open. His helmet was full of snow.

Ada turned around and shouted back towards the tent. The woman who had spoken to her was the first to reach her.

"I found Masha," Ada said, as she approached.

"It can't be him," the woman said. "This is not where the avalanche fell."

Together they dug out the rest of the body. More people gathered around. Ada's mother helped her pull the body out and lay it on the packed snow. When she saw the face, she screamed.

"It's Atticus," Ada said to her father. "It's Atticus."

"That's not possible," her father said. "He was with us this morning. He said he was going back to the hotel."

"It's him," her mother said. "Look at his face. It's him. He must have hit a tree."

"Oh, my god," her father said. "I don't know what we're going to do."

"My son," her mother said. "My only child. It's not possible."

ADA FOUND THE door, standing improbably on the edge of the hillside, and went back through it.

Atticus was everywhere. Her parents had a life before her, she thought. She pictured them again, dancing together in front of a fire, surrounded by a crowd of strangers. They had loved each other once. That's where I am, Ada thought, held in the space between them as they dance in front of the fire. The problem was that she had continued to exist after they stopped loving each other, and now she had no place, only the ghost of Atticus filling in for it, multiplying like a virus that corrupted everything she tried to want.

She remembered all the times she had heard the voice, whispering in her ear, telling her things that she should never have known. She had assumed that Don had chosen the information and transmitted it to her, but she really had no way of knowing. It could be that the facility wanted to share what it knew. Perhaps it was trying to tell her something, to make a connection that she didn't have the capacity to understand. Ada was frustrated. Whatever it was that the facility was supposed to do, it wasn't working. She didn't want Atticus, whether he was a tiger or a dead man in a ski resort, but she didn't know how to stop wanting him.

There was somebody standing in the corridor. The lights were still dim and it took Ada a moment to realize that it was Don.

"Ada," he said. "Are you okay?"

"How did you know I was here?"

"It seemed like you were in trouble," he said. He paused, and then continued, as if he knew what she would ask. "If something goes wrong, we can all feel it."

"It doesn't seem to go both ways," Ada said. "I can't feel anybody else."

"That's because you don't fully understand how it works. It takes time."

"You're watching me," Ada said. "It's still an experiment."

"No," Don said. "We want to help you."

"I made a person," Ada said, "and then when I didn't want him anymore, I killed him. I went into a room and it was just playing on a screen, over and over."

"It was what you wanted. There's nothing to be ashamed of in that."

"That's not right," Ada said. "He was a person. People don't stop existing when you don't want them anymore."

"You have to give in to it," Don said. "Or you'll never be whole. You can't deny yourself the things you want forever. You can't keep feeling guilty and ashamed."

"I'm not more important than anybody else," Ada said.

"You're the most important person to yourself."

"You look caring, but really you're selfish. You don't believe that other people are real." Don looked down. Ada couldn't tell if he was angry with her or if she had hurt him. She wondered, obscurely, if she was part of what he wanted. "Why is Atticus everywhere?" she asked.

Don took a long time before answering.

"Do you really want to know?" he said.

"Yes. That's what I want."

"We made him, the same way we made you."

"But I met him before I came here."

"That's not what I mean. You come from the same place. We made you from the same material. You were never meant to meet. It recognized itself." He paused. "That's why we had to give you a new body. Your connection was compromising the experiment."

"You made me?"

"There was no other way. We had to build you with the implant already inside."

"But my mother gave birth to me."

"There are ways," Don said. "To provide the base material. You wouldn't understand." Ada looked at him. She imagined a shard of glass impaling him through one of his pale blue eyes. Atticus was her, and she was him. Everything she had thought had been true. Don had lied to her.

"I hate you," she said. "I want to go home."

Part 4

Ada's replacement flew home alone. The airport was too air-conditioned and the plastic chair she sat on left red lines on the back of her bare arms and legs.

She had packed a suitcase while her mother sat silently on the patio. When Ada said goodbye, she had refused to look at her. Instead she examined the cracked tiles, between which small green shoots grew in neat lines. Ada had walked to the village and taken the evening ferry. On the other side, she called a taxi to take her to the airport. She spent the night on the plastic chair before taking the earliest flight back to London.

Her father called her while she was waiting at the gate.

"I've been thinking about it," he said. "What we talked about. I don't want you to think I don't care about you."

"I know," Ada said.

"I just find it difficult," he said, "the way you handle these things. You don't tell me what you're doing, and then you ring me up afterwards to help when there's nothing I can do to help you."

"It's okay," Ada said. "You don't need to help me."

"Have you worked things out with your mother?"

"I'm coming home." Ada paused. "She won't speak to me."

He didn't say anything for a moment. Ada watched a small Greek boy playing alone by the large window. There was a circle of blue beads, a souvenir from the beach, around his chubby brown wrist. Outside a plane was landing, and he stopped playing for a moment to watch, pressing his small hands against the glass.

"It won't last," her father said, finally. "She loves you."

"Can I come and stay with you?" The question took her by surprise. She didn't know she was going to ask it until the words had already left her mouth. The thought of her apartment, waiting for her like an empty, discarded shell, made her feel tired. She didn't want to go back to anything that she already knew.

"I don't know," her father said. "I don't know where you'd sleep."

"I can sleep on the sofa."

"Okay," her father said. There was a long silence.

"What're you thinking?" she asked.

"You've never lived with me," he said. "I don't know why."

"You didn't want me to," Ada said.

"That's true," he said. "I don't know why I didn't. I think I didn't want you to need me. I thought you'd just be like your mother." He paused again. "When will you be here?"

"Tonight," Ada said. "My flight arrives at five."

"Okay," he said. "I'll see you then."

They said goodbye and hung up.

On the airplane, she was calm. Thinking about her mother was like watching a storm unfold from behind a glass window. Ada knew that what had happened was her fault. Her behavior on the holiday had been strange and distant. The whole of the past month had been like a dream, like walking underwater.

Now her head was clear. On the flight, she looked out the window. Her thoughts moved in an orderly parade—she could almost see them bouncing past on the soft, white clouds, one at a time. Now that she was free of her apartment, she looked forward to what awaited her at home. Her father's house was small and comfortable. Francesca was coming to pick her up from the airport. They had spoken on the phone briefly when Ada called her from the taxi. Francesca seemed surprised and relieved to hear from her. Ada wasn't sure why they hadn't spoken in such a long time.

The plane was landing. Her stomach rolled over. The man beside her was reading a book, a large hardback with a colorful cover. She asked him what it was. He shifted in his seat to face her when he answered.

"It's about the brain," he said. "How it learns new things. They used to think it reached maturity and everything was fixed, but it's plastic. It keeps changing until we die."

Ada gripped the armrests.

"Are you scared of flying?" the man asked.

"I don't like landing," she said. Outside the window, the rooftops of London lurched into view. The man turned back to his book. He wore a smart white shirt. "Where are you from?" she asked him.

"Abidjan."

"Where is that?"

"Ivory Coast."

Earlier on in the flight the attendants had brought around a selection of complimentary snacks and drinks. Ada noticed that the man had left his packet of pretzels and sparkling water untouched. She thought about asking if she could have them. The plane tilted again, and she closed her eyes tightly. Her stomach was turning over on itself, and she had a terrible pain in her ears, as if her head was splitting open from the inside.

They landed. The man said goodbye to her before he disappeared into the baggage-claim area. He gave her a slip of paper on which he'd written the name of the book, which Ada put in her pocket. As she watched him go, she regretted not asking him more about himself.

Francesca was waiting for her at arrivals. Her blonde hair hung loose around her pale face. She was wearing the same shiny green coat. Unlike Ada, she could drive and owned a car. Ada hugged her. She felt Francesca's body sag. When she stepped back, she saw that her cousin's eyes were wet.

"What's wrong?" Ada asked.

"I thought you hated me," Francesca said.

"I don't hate you," Ada said. "I love you."

They left the airport and found the car. It was small and clean. Ada put her bag on the back seat. London was an hour's drive away. She didn't mention that she was going to her father's. After a moment she realized it was because she didn't know the address.

"What happened?" Francesca asked.

"I don't know," Ada said. "Mum asked me to go to Greece with her. When I got there everything was strange. We didn't know how to talk to each other. Now she won't talk to me at all."

"Why didn't you tell me you were leaving?"

"I saw you in the restaurant, with Carlo."

Francesca went quiet. They drove in silence for a while. It was still early in the morning, and the sun was just beginning to warm the damp gray rooftops that connected the airport to the suburbs of London.

"I didn't mean for anything to happen," Francesca said, after a while. "He gave me his number. I went back to the restaurant after I was sure that you'd gone. I was so upset about Eric. I thought about telling you." She stopped.

"What happened?" Ada asked.

"He started making me drinks. He said he thought that I was beautiful. I didn't even like him. I was just happy that somebody was interested in me. He kissed me. His hands were all sweaty and his face was red. I couldn't stop thinking how he looked like a baby, with the sweaty collar of his polo shirt sticking up. After I went home, he kept calling me until I turned off my phone."

"I was jealous when I saw you," Ada said.

"I don't know why," Francesca said. "There's something wrong with me."

For a while they drove in silence. As Ada looked out the window at the lines of brown and gray buildings, she wished that Francesca didn't always have to be so honest.

"Have you seen Patrick?"

"No," Francesca said. "He called to ask me about you."

"What did you say?"

"I thought it was the old man. I said you'd probably run away with him."

"I haven't been a very good friend," Ada said.

"It's okay," Francesca said. "Neither have I."

ADA LET FRANCESCA take her back to her apartment. She didn't want to admit that she didn't know where her father lived, and she didn't want to call him and ask in front of Francesca. When they arrived at Ada's building, Francesca carried her bag up the stairs. Ada opened the windows of her studio and straightened out the bed. Everything had been left a mess. Francesca stood in the kitchen and said nothing while Ada beat the pillows back into a respectable shape. There were mugs that had been left in the sink, now covered in mold. Ada turned on her phone. There was nothing from her mother.

"Why did you leave it like this?" Francesca asked. "Were you depressed?"

"I can't remember," Ada said. "I was scared of something, but now it's gone, and I can't remember what it was."

"Was it because of that man?" Francesca asked.

"I was in love with him," Ada said. "He went back to California without telling me." The door to the bathroom was open. The light was on. Inside, Ada saw something on the floor beneath the sink. It was a snow drift of tissues, stained brown with old blood. She collected them and put them in the bin. It disturbed her that she couldn't remember where they had come from, and that she'd left the light on for the better part of two weeks. Perhaps somebody had broken in, but nothing was missing.

She knew that her cousin was watching her. Ada didn't understand why. She went back into the main room.

"Is everything okay?" Ada asked.

"Yes," Francesca said. "I have to go." She was standing by the door, her bag in her hand. It was made of cracked reddish leather, the same color as the stained tissues, that stood out against her green coat like the open mouth of a crocodile.

"Okay," Ada said. Francesca lingered for a moment longer, as if waiting for Ada to say something else. Then she turned and left.

Ada called her father and asked for his address. He gave it to her and asked what she would like to do that evening. She said she wanted to go out for dinner and he suggested somewhere near his house. She would meet him at the restaurant in two hours.

She was glad to be alone. She emptied her bag and put the wrinkled clothes into the washing machine. Then she sat down on the edge of the bed. What would she do next? She could walk around the park and listen to the birds singing, or climb into bed and sleep until she was ready to wake up, dreaming about nothing. The first thing she did was go into the bathroom and begin to run herself a bath. While it filled up, she cleaned. With vinegar and newspapers, she wiped down the windows and mirrors until no streak or fingerprint remained. She swept the floors, and then mopped them, then shuffled around with an old towel beneath her feet until they were dry and gleaming. When she was finished, her apartment looked like some kind of showroom. In her enthusiasm, she had even wiped down the dusty, browning leaves of her potted plants in the hope of somewhat reviving them. She wanted to leave it behind in a pristine state, so that she would never have to think about it again. She didn't think about how she would pay the rent. When the bath was full, she turned off the taps, and now it sat waiting for her, populating the room with steam.

She got in, but something was wrong. Looking down, she realized that she had forgotten to take off her clothes.

ADA LOOKED AT her father. Every time she saw him it seemed impossible that he could get bigger, but still he continued to grow. He wore a shirt that looked several sizes too small. Beneath his collar Ada noticed that his chest and neck were sunburnt. He had gone somewhere on holiday. Ada didn't ask him where.

They were in the restaurant. Ada had drained the bath and put her wet clothes in the dryer, along with the contents of the washing machine. Whatever was left in the cupboard she had packed into a cloth bag to take with her. She imagined she was shedding her skin. She had the feeling that it was something she had imagined many times before, and so it lost its meaning.

In between Ada and her father stood an open bottle of water. Neither of them had ordered other drinks. Ada's father did not drink alcohol. The tablecloth was very white. Ada found herself staring at the creases, where crumbs and other detritus collected.

Her father asked her how she was.

"I don't know," Ada said. "Mum hasn't spoken to me since I left Greece."

She saw her father's face tighten.

"I don't want to hear about it," he said. "You need to figure these things out on your own."

"I know," Ada said. "I only brought it up because I haven't been thinking about it at all."

On the way to the restaurant, she had dropped her bag off at his house. He had cleared his bodybuilding equipment to one end of the living room so that the space around the sofa was free. The room was dark and had a strange, musty smell. He kept the curtains closed. The kitchen was cluttered with plates and cutlery, clean, but not put away. None of it made Ada consider going back to her apartment. She would rather sleep on the floor than face a night alone in her large white bed. She needed to be with someone, to know that somebody was aware of her presence. Francesca was too unhappy. Ada could feel it infecting her, like a virus. Only her father remained unmoved.

Her father didn't reply for a minute. He picked up the menu and looked at it. Ada looked back down at the tablecloth, then towards the window. Outside, the street was dark and full of people.

"There's been too many fights," her father said. "I don't want to hear about fighting. Other things have to happen to you. What your mother thinks can't control your life."

"Something is happening to me," Ada said. "After we had the fight, I just left. I've barely thought about it."

"Tell me about something else. Tell me about your job."

"I have an empty life," Ada said. Her father looked at her across the table.

"Sometimes," he said, "you make me feel like a terrible person."

The waiter came over. Ada looked at the menu. She ordered something random, not fully understanding what it was. Her father ordered a steak and a salad.

"Are you on steroids?" she asked.

"No," he said.

"Did you ever have an affair?"

"No," he said. "Why are you asking me?"

"I don't feel like I know you at all," Ada said. "You're a stranger."

"Your mother kept us apart," he said.

"But you left," Ada said. "And you never call me. You could call me whenever you want." Her father looked away. Ada could see that there were lines on his face. She imagined her own face covered in wrinkles, far in the future, when both her mother and her father were dead.

"Ada," her father said. "I'm sorry you had a fight. You have to find a way of working these things out inside yourself, so it doesn't affect your whole life."

"It doesn't affect me at all," Ada said.

"It's good," her father said, "that you're staying with me."

"I tried to tell you what was going on," she said.

"Is all of this really because of your mother?"

"I don't know," Ada said. "I don't know what's wrong with me."

"You want to be in control," her father said, "but being in control means taking responsibility, and you don't want to do that. You can't control people by being weak." He looked down at the tablecloth. On the top of his head, his red hair was thinning.

"That's not a reason," Ada said.

"Well then," her father said, "I don't know what to tell you."

The waiter brought their food. Ada had ordered badly. On her plate sat several pieces of meat she didn't recognize, swimming in a watery red sauce that looked like blood. She had no appetite. They had given her a serrated knife, but she couldn't use it. The pieces of meat on her plate looked too vulnerable. Her father ate his salad delicately. The steak sat beside his elbow. Ada wondered how he ate so little and still maintained his grotesque body.

"You're a happy person," her father said, as if he'd been thinking about it for some time. "You always were happy."

"I'm not happy," Ada said. "I'm angry."

"What're you angry about?"

"I want to know what happened before you moved out."

Her father was silent. Ada picked up the serrated knife. The dim light caught on it. Holding it tightly, she imagined driving it into her father's face. She felt calm.

"I'm going to tell you something," her father said. He paused.

"Okay."

"There were times," he said, "when your mother thought that you didn't belong to us." He paused again. He had put his fork down and held a piece of bread delicately between his fingers. Ada tried to imagine what it was like to be him. She knew that if she had ever made him feel needed, he would have been there, but instead she had needed her mother more than anyone. "She was suspicious of you. She thought that you weren't real, that you didn't come from her."

Ada looked at the wall behind her father's head. It was a deep blue. She imagined that it was the sea, and that she was diving into it, deeper and deeper, until everything on the surface disappeared.

"Does she still think that?"

"I don't know," her father said. "It wasn't all the time, just when other things were stressful."

"But you left me with her."

"You made her miserable, but she refused to let you go. She still loved you a lot. It was very confusing for her. She cried all the time, and I couldn't help her."

"In Greece, she said that she didn't know who I was."

"I'm sorry." Ada looked at her father. His face was red. He took a sip from his water glass. She realized, as she thought about what he'd said, that she had already known. The idea had always been with her, dodging out of sight whenever she turned her head, but there, nonetheless. Her mother did not really believe in her existence.

"I hate you," she said. It surprised her that she had said it, because it wasn't true. She just wanted her father to know what he had done by leaving.

"I know," he said. He stopped eating. He looked pale and sad. "I think that you should come to the gym."

SHE WENT WITH him the next day. The gym was crowded and bright. It smelled of sweat and chalk and was warm with human proximity. Ada's father gave her weights to hold, small for a beginner, and showed her how to lift them with the correct form. He said he would make her a plan for improvement. For the first time she became aware of how weak her body really was.

She had spent an uncomfortable night on the sofa. Her father didn't sleep very much, and she could hear him walking around the house, turning the lights on and off, watching television in his bedroom. She knew that she was inconveniencing him. The gym equipment he had collected over the years surrounded her like a display of bizarre and beautiful sculptures. They hadn't spoken much after dinner. Ada knew her father felt guilty. He had let her down, and it was up to her whether or not she would forgive him. It was useless to try to make him understand what he had done by leaving her in her mother's house, because he already knew, and he could do nothing to change it.

Late at night she called her mother, knowing that she wouldn't pick up. Listening to it ring out, she became acutely aware of how unfamiliar the room was, full of her father's things, which she had never seen. It was like being inside his head. There was a poster on the wall that showed a photograph of an orange tree, with a woman standing beneath it, holding a basket of oranges in her arms. Ada wondered where he had gotten it. Maybe someone had given it to him—a friend or a girlfriend. Ada doubted he had either.

In the gym there was a full-length mirror along one wall. Ada looked at herself. Her skin was very pale, and her hair was brown. There were dark circles beneath her eyes. Her arms and legs were soft and round, mottled with a red flush. The skin on her face wasn't smooth, but it wasn't noticeably marked with acne or scarring. She was medium height, and medium weight. Only her eyes stood out, oddly spherical, close together, and full of rage. No men looked in her direction as she followed her father's instructions. They looked at him, at his tight shirt stained with dark sweat, his face red and bulging.

Today he was focusing on his arms. He worked hard and with intense concentration. If Ada tried to speak to him, he wouldn't hear what she was saying. Several times she tried to ask if they could stop, but he went on lifting weights until it seemed to Ada like he might burst. When he finally put them down, he was sweating so hard he might as well have been out in the rain. Ada was sweating too. The pale skin of her cheeks had a pink flush. She liked the way it made her look.

Her father sat down to rest. Ada could see his veins straining against his muscles.

"What do I look like?" she asked him.

"There's a mirror right in front of you."

"I feel like I can never really see myself."

"I only started seeing myself when I started going to the gym. Before that I was invisible. Now I feel like I have a strong outline, and people can see me."

"What happens if you get injured, and you have to stop going?"

"That would be something else," he said. "I'd be somebody who used to be fit, and had become unfit. I still wouldn't be nothing."

"One day you'll be old," Ada said.

"I don't mind," he said. "I just told you. Taking it away doesn't set things back to zero."

When they were done, she went into the bathroom to wash her hands. The water ran hot. Looking in the bathroom mirror she tried to discern which parts of her face had come from her mother and which from her father.

"Do you still feel angry?" her father asked her when she came back out.

"Yes," she said.

While she was waiting for him to pack up his things a woman approached her. She was about the age of Ada's father, with gray hair, but not as well-built.

"Are you his daughter?" she asked Ada. "Lucas's?"

"No," Ada said. She had forgotten that her father had a name.

"Oh," the woman said. She paused for a moment, as if she didn't know what to say. "I'm Sandy," she said. There was another pause. Ada looked at the gray floor. "How do you know him?"

"He's adopting me."

"That's great," Sandy said. "I just know he has a daughter, so I thought you might be her."

"I'll be his daughter soon," Ada said. Sandy nodded, as if she understood. She had a tattoo on her arm of a purple flower. Ada thought it looked like an open wound, or a vagina.

Her father came back from the changing room. He had his bag over his shoulder and a blue plastic water bottle in his hand. Ada looked at Sandy to see if she would say anything. She looked apprehensive, as if she was worried that Ada was playing a joke on her. Ada wanted to ask her what was wrong, to reassure her that she was telling the truth, but her father was already speaking.

"Sandy," he said. "I'll see you next time."

Ada stood beside him, suddenly unsure if he could see her. She looked for some proof in his face, but it was red and blank. She looked at Sandy, but Sandy had turned away. Even her reflection in the mirror was like a stranger. The noise of the gym faded away until she was standing in a bubble of her own breath. She worried that she would run out of air and choke. Then her father said that it was time to go, and the bubble burst.

WHEN THEY GOT home, her arms were painful. Lying on the sofa, she tried to remember what she looked like. Usually she struggled to picture her own face, but this time it came easily. She saw herself, her dry brown hair in a braid, face decorated with fair skin and round piggish eyes, her snub nose, the small earrings she never took out, the freckle beside her mouth, her slightly discolored teeth. There she was, a complete image.

It didn't last long. Her father had disappeared to make a phone call. His work was freelance so that he had more time for bodybuilding. It occurred to Ada that while she had always imagined both her parents as wealthy, she didn't know if it was true of her father. The phone call was the first work she'd seen him do. The workout equipment must have cost money, she thought. She wondered where it came from, and then decided that it didn't matter.

She wondered what she would do to make money. She had no job and was meant to be paying rent on her apartment.

There was nothing she was particularly good at, nothing she could imagine doing every day for the rest of her life. It was like time had stopped. She looked at the ceiling, textured like popcorn, painted pale beige. The light bulb in the overhead lampshade was dusty and ringed with cobwebs. She could go back to the restaurant, but she didn't want to see Carlo. Her father's voice slipped under the door from the kitchen. He was talking about something she didn't understand, something to do with computers. Outside the window, the yellow light told her it was late in the afternoon. Looking at the heavy curtains, she thought that her mother was right. She was like an empty tin can, full of nothing.

When her father opened the door, she realized she had fallen asleep.

"You should go for a walk," he said.

"Will you come with me?"

"No," he said.

"Then I don't want to." He stood in the doorway, casting a shadow across the carpet.

"Come and sit in the kitchen," he said.

He had put away the clean dishes. The narrow floor was tiled with terra-cotta squares. There was a folding card table with two plastic chairs tucked beneath it. On it there was a wooden bowl with a bunch of yellow bananas and a ring of keys. Ada pulled out a chair and sat down.

"Have you talked to your mother?" he asked.

"I don't know what to say to her."

"As long as you can keep it up on the surface, things will sort themselves out. You can talk about it when things are normal again."

"I want her to apologize."

"I'm sure she feels the same way." He looked down at his wide, flat thumbs, resting on the plastic countertop. Again, Ada saw where his hair was thinning.

"She doesn't think that I'm real."

"That doesn't mean that you're not."

"Yes it does," Ada said. "Of course it does."

"Maybe you're right," he said. "She didn't believe in you, and now you don't believe in yourself, but you're real to me, and you belong to me. I can see you. You're a person to me."

THE NEXT DAY they went back to the gym. In the night, Ada had dreamt that she was pulling something out of the earth. She pulled with all her strength until her arms burned and it felt like they would come loose at the sockets. When she looked down to see what she was tugging at, she saw a pair of pale hands, covered in dirt, that she recognized as her own.

The gym was the same. Her father worked on his legs. He sat on a machine and pushed a stack of weights with his feet. There was only one machine, so Ada walked on a treadmill. She could barely lift her arms. They felt soft and pliable, like melting plastic.

Sandy wasn't there. When men came up to greet Ada's father, he didn't introduce them to Ada. She wondered if he was ashamed of her because she was so weak. When he stopped to rest, she went up to him.

"Why don't you tell them who I am?" she asked.

"I didn't think you'd want to meet them," he said. He paused. "You need to eat more protein," he said.

She went back to the treadmill. There was a television screen on the wall in front of her. A game show was playing. All the questions seemed impossible, and yet the man on the screen got each one right. Ada watched as the number representing the amount of money he had won ticked up. Finally, the presenter asked a question that made him pause and look briefly down at his hands. When he answered, the green button turned red, and the number reset to zero. Ada expected him to react with anger but he smiled a bashful smile, as if he was just happy to have had the chance. The question that he had been unable to answer rang around her head: "After the great flood, Noah sent out two birds of different types from the Ark. Which two types of birds were they?" The presenter, after a moment, revealed the answer: "The dove and the raven."

It seemed a strange question to stumble on. Ada looked over at her father. He had moved to a corner of the gym and was doing squats with weights in his hands. She remembered the first time he came home after going to the gym. It had been one of his colleagues who had introduced him to it. He had been slim and slightly frail, but good-looking, with his red hair and blue eyes. After coming home, he had been quiet at dinner. When Ada's mother asked him why, he had said that he was tired, something that always made her upset.

"You don't make an effort," she'd said. Ada remembered her blonde hair falling down around her shoulders.

"I'm making an effort," her father had said, "for myself."

After that, he was separated from Ada and her mother, as if an invisible wall had come down between them. For a year they lived in an in-between state, where he and her mother slept in separate bedrooms, until eventually he left completely.

"I've been neglecting my own needs," she had heard him tell her mother, on the day he moved out. "I have to put myself and my bodybuilding first."

It was that night that Ada had thrown herself down the stairs and broken her wrist.

She was standing outside the building waiting for her father when she felt somebody touch her arm. It was a gray day, and drizzle dampened her hair and jacket. Turning around in surprise, she saw Patrick. In his hand was a plastic shopping bag.

"Ada. You're crying."

"No I'm not," she said. She looked down and saw that the neck of her shirt was wet. It was pale yellow. She couldn't remember putting it on.

"Come with me," he said. "Come with me." He put an arm around her shoulders. Ada realized she couldn't remember the last time somebody had touched her. It surprised her that he tried, after what had happened the last time. This time she didn't mind, and she felt that somehow, he knew. His hand clasped her shoulder firmly. He led her to a bench where they sat down. He put his shopping bag on the ground. Ada saw that it contained several large oranges. "What're you doing here?" he asked.

"I'm waiting for my father," she said. "He's on the phone." She wiped her face on her sleeve. "We went to the gym."

"Why are you crying?"

"I thought I would feel better, but I don't."

"Of course you don't," Patrick said. "It's ridiculous."

"Exercise is meant to make you feel better."

They were sitting on a bench in the parking lot. People walked past them, occasionally glancing at Ada's wet, red face and stained shirt. Patrick sat close to her but didn't touch her again. His hands were in his pockets.

"I think it only works for some people," he said. Ada looked at him.

"Really?"

"I think so."

"I wanted to be closer with my father," she said. "But I feel further away."

"That makes sense," Patrick said. They sat for a moment in silence.

"I didn't go away because of the old man," Ada said. "I know that's what Francesca told you, but it wasn't true. I went on holiday with my mother." He nodded.

"I thought it couldn't be that," he said. "It didn't seem like the type of thing you'd do."

"How do you know?"

"I think I know you," he said.

"There isn't anything to know," Ada said.

"The most interesting things about other people," he said, "are the things they don't know about themselves, the things only other people can see."

Leaning over, with the gray sun silhouetted behind his head, he kissed her. His mouth was warm. When he pulled away, Ada felt dampness on her lips. A bus stopped behind them and people began to get off, parting around the bench they sat on. It seemed to Ada like the world was suddenly more populated than it had been moments ago. Patrick was about to say something when Ada heard her father behind her.

"Ada," he said. "Are you ready to go?" She turned around. He had changed into clean clothes. They were baggy, and hid the bulk of his body. Only his neck was visible, veins still swollen with exertion.

"This is Patrick," she said. "My friend. I'm going to stay here with him." Her father nodded.

"Okay," he said, "I'll see you later." His gym bag was on his shoulder. In his hand was a red plastic water bottle. Ada watched him walk away down the gray street. A woman in a fur coat glanced at him as she passed. Ada turned back to Patrick.

"What were you going to say?" she asked.

"That you should stay here with me," he said.

PATRICK'S BEDROOM WAS strangely bare. There was a mattress on the floor covered by a colorful blanket. In one corner there was a desk, empty apart from a lamp, and a chair that had been dragged in from the kitchen. An open suitcase in the other corner held his clothes. When Ada asked him how long it'd been since he'd moved in, he said two years. Between the desk and the bed there was a matted green rug, thick and square, stretched across the concrete floor.

Patrick's hand was resting on her shoulder. Ada imagined herself a porcelain sculpture, smooth and cool. Only her shoulders and her feet protruded from the blanket.

"I thought I'd never see you again," he said. "After last time."

"I'm sorry," Ada said.

"Don't apologize," he said. "When I saw you outside the gym, I knew that something had changed. It was like you were in this big glass bubble, and now it's broken open." He paused. "It's like there's two of you."

"I don't feel different," Ada said. "Is it because I was crying?"

"Maybe."

"My father left my mother because she cried too much."

"Maybe he shouldn't have made her cry."

"He couldn't help it," Ada said. "It's just who he is. He's selfish."

Patrick lived in a large brick building. From the outside, the lights of the windows had looked like fireflies in a dark garden. They had walked there all the way from the gym. It had taken them two hours. Patrick sometimes read the names of shops they passed, but most of the walk had been in silence. The rain made both of them wet and cold, but he didn't seem to mind.

When they arrived, he gave her some of his clothes to wear and hung up her wet clothes on the radiator. There was nobody else home, although he said he lived with three other people. His attentiveness made Ada sad. She wished that he would stop, so that she would be forced to collect herself and make an effort. As it was, she kept crying. The well inside her felt infinitely deep. Patrick made spaghetti while she sat on the old, sagging sofa. The faded red fabric made her nostalgic, but she didn't know what for. She thought about her grandparents' house, where she had occasionally spent the weekend as a child. They had lived on an old farm in the countryside, near the sea, with raspberry canes in the garden. Ada remembered eating the raspberries straight off the spiny bushes. Once, she had stepped on a wasp and her foot had swollen up. Her grandmother had covered it in ashes and wrapped it in newspaper, and the swelling had gone away.

The roof of the house had been partially burnt when she was seventeen, after her grandmother left a candle lit in the attic. Now both of her grandparents lived in a nursing home. Ada knew her father went to see them every other weekend, but she had never gone with him, because he had never asked her to. She had sent them a postcard, once, from university, with a drawing of the building that she lived in.

She and Patrick ate sitting side by side on the sofa. She had finally stopped crying, and they had gone to bed.

She asked Patrick why he wanted to take care of her. He laughed and moved his hand back under the blanket, where it lay coolly against her back.

"I like taking care of people," he said. "I'm just that kind of person."

"How do you know how to do it?"

"I thought about what I'd want if I were you."

"I don't know what I'd want," she said, "if I were you." There was a patch of cracked plaster on the wall that made the shape of a hand.

"I've been seeing someone. It just ended. I thought she was something that I wanted, but she was a little disinterested in everything. At the end I felt like I could have turned her over and shaken her like a piggy bank and nothing else would've come out."

"What was she like?"

"She goes out into the woods to listen to nightingales. I went with her once."

It seemed like it was impossible not to love Patrick. His curly hair stood out from around his pale face. His body was firm and compact, but his hands were soft and delicate. The tattoo on his shoulder looked up at her like a black eye. In the comfort of his room, she waited to fall in love with him, but all she felt was a blank gray fog, as if everything had been covered in a layer of felt.

She slept badly. The mattress was uncomfortable, and the room was hot and unventilated. When they woke up, she had a headache. They stayed in bed, listening to Patrick's housemates move around in the kitchen. Ada had heard them come back, late in the night. She wondered if they knew she was there. She listened to the voices, their laughing, and she wished that they would go so that she could leave. In the corner of her eye, she was aware of Patrick looking at her.

"I need to go," she said.

He kissed her shoulder with his soft, dry mouth.

"I hope you come back," he said.

Upon leaving, she was surprised by her own blitheness. It was still early in the morning. Suspended in the gray fog of exhaustion, on the way home she barely thought about him, but in her body, there was a feeling of warmth and satisfaction, as if she'd swallowed a hot stone.

Her father called her and asked when she was coming back.

"I'm not," she said. "I'm going back to my apartment."

"I'm worried about you," he said. "Exercise helps everything. You need to look after your body."

"I don't need it anymore," she said.

"Give it a chance," he said. "Come back one more time."

Ada hung up the phone. She didn't want to have to become like her father for him to understand her. When she got back to her apartment she opened the curtains, letting in the full force of the sun.

HER APARTMENT WAS quiet and still. The plants had turned yellow. She tried to call Francesca but it rang out with no answer. As she listened to it ring, she imagined a voice talking to her. It sounded like her own, but it was very far away. She imagined it trying to capture her attention, but she ignored it, focusing instead on the repetitive sound of Francesca's ringtone. It got louder, until it was shouting at her, demanding that she listen. Ada was surprised by how real it sounded. She could almost believe that there was a real person on the other end, stuck somewhere she couldn't see, calling out to her through the phone line. She was about to reply when it cut to Francesca's voicemail, and she hung up without leaving a message.

For the first time since leaving Greece she missed her mother acutely. She imagined her sitting alone on the beach, dry blonde hair loose around her shoulders, looking out over the water. Just as she thought it, her phone lit up in her hand. She looked down. Like in a dream, it was her mother calling her. Ada stared at the screen. Then she answered.

For a moment neither of them spoke.

"I know what you think," Ada said. "You think that I'm not real."

Her mother took a long time to reply. Ada listened to the silence, and imagined her mother breathing, in and out, waiting until she knew what to say.

"Did your father tell you that?" It was strange to hear her voice.

"Yes," Ada said. "But I knew it already." She was sitting at the table in her kitchen. There was a fine layer of dust on the surface, almost invisible until she pushed her finger through it and revealed the darker surface beneath.

"I just didn't see," her mother said, pausing between each word, "how you could be mine." Her voice was somehow stale and electric at the same time.

"Why not?"

"We're not the same."

"You don't want me," Ada said. Anger spread across her skin like a hot rash. After saying it she realized that she should have asked if they were meant to be the same, but she knew how her mother would answer: yes.

"It's not that," her mother said. "That's not true at all. It's the opposite. I love you. But even when you were a baby, you didn't belong to me. I could feel it in my heart. I felt that you hated me."

"Why?"

"I don't know," her mother said. "I never knew what to do." She paused. "I felt that you preferred your father."

"I know," Ada said. She remembered what her mother had said in Greece, that honesty was overrated, and wondered if she would prefer her mother to lie. Her words were like a paring knife, separating the rind from the flesh, or the meat from the bone. What they left behind was like a skeleton. It made Ada feel cold.

"It just seemed like if you were going to be mine, you would be all mine. I didn't know how I was supposed to cope with sharing you."

Ada went into the bathroom. Still holding the phone, she got into the bathtub and with one hand turned on the hot tap. Warm water ran over her feet.

"You mean with Dad," she said.

"I guess so," her mother said. "I didn't know it clearly until after he left. I just knew that you weren't all *mine*."

"I was still half yours."

"Half is the same as nothing."

"I know."

"I love you," her mother said. "I don't know what's wrong with me. It's not your fault."

"I love you too." Silently, Ada started to cry. She watched the tears fall into the water that swirled around her feet. "Do you remember when you used to go and stand on the beach?"

"Yes."

"Why did you do that?"

"I was too scared to be in the house."

"Because of me?"

"Because of your father." Ada didn't reply. She didn't want to ask why her mother had been scared. Inside her she felt a door swing shut. "I have to go," her mother said. Ada's silent tears fell harder, splashing into the bath like rain. "I'm in a restaurant. I'll call you tomorrow. We can talk about this more."

"I don't want to talk about it anymore."

The line went silent. There was a strange feeling in Ada's chest, as if what was inside was being pulled outside of her. Suddenly she felt very cold. The hot water barely made a difference. She stayed in the bath until the water was nearly up to her neck. She could feel it burning her, but she still felt cold.

She hugged her knees to her chest. Her clothes were heavy. She told herself that nothing had changed, that her mother had only told the truth, but it felt as if every bit of heat had been rinsed from the world. Looking at the tiles on the floor, she wondered if there had been any to begin with. She closed her eyes and leaned back against the lip of the bathtub. Her phone was on the floor. She heard it ring, and waited a moment before picking it up, but when she leaned over the edge of the bath and looked at the screen it was black and silent.

She heard the voice again, calling out to her. It was asking for another chance. Ignoring it, she stayed in the bath until the water was cold, and she began to shiver.

THE NEXT AFTERNOON Patrick came to meet her at her door. In his hand was a bouquet of yellow carnations. Although she had her coat and shoes on, Ada went back inside to find a glass of water to put them in.

"I've never bought anybody flowers before," he said. He was standing in the doorway. Ada found a jar and put the flowers on the kitchen table.

"Thank you," she said.

They were going for a walk. Patrick had called in the morning to ask. As they left the building, he asked her if she would have eventually called him, and she said that she didn't know. He laughed, as if he knew that she would have. There was a canal that ran all the way from behind Ada's building to the center of the city. They had planned to walk the entire length of the overgrown footpath. Dilapidated houseboats and plastic bottles swam in the oily water. Occasionally a family of moorhens with bright yellow feet passed them by. Ada asked Patrick how he was.

"I'm well," he said.

"What happened with your play?"

"It didn't really go anywhere," he said. "Now I'm working on a new project, a collection of short stories."

"Oh," Ada said. "I'm sorry."

"Don't be," he said. They walked for a while in silence. It was just cold enough for both of them to keep their hands in their pockets.

"I had a dream," Ada said, "last night. I heard my own voice coming from the radio in my kitchen. It said that there was another version of me, somewhere else. She said that she was the first one, and that I was only a replacement."

"What do you think it means?" Patrick asked.

"In the dream it seemed like she was stuck, and she wanted me to help her, but I just got up and turned off the radio." Ada paused. They stepped to the side to allow a cyclist to pass. He was wearing colorful Lycra that seemed out of place beside the gray canal. "Last night my mother told me that she thinks I'm not real."

"What?"

"She thinks that I belong to someone else. She always did, even when I was a baby."

"And you didn't know?"

"No."

"I'm sorry."

"We had a fight in Greece," Ada said. "I came home without her." She watched a brown duck dip its head under the oily water. "I feel guilty about it," she said.

"Where does she think you came from?"

"I don't know."

They walked in silence for a while. Patrick walked with his head bowed, as if there was a heavy weight pressing down on the back of his neck.

"It's relatively common," he said, after a while.

"What is?"

"Thinking that people in your life are impostors." Ada didn't respond. Her heart was beating fast, as if she were running down the path instead of walking. "Sometimes I think being close with your parents is harder than hating them," he said. "I knew I hated my parents from the time I was twelve. I see them once a year on Christmas, and the rest of the time I never think about them at all."

"How do you cope with making them sad?"

"It's awful." He paused. "It's not true that I never think about them. I think about them all the time, and how much they must miss me."

"Do you miss them?"

"No." They walked on. There were houses along the canal, newly built. Through the windows Ada could see rooms with smooth wooden floors and clean white walls. All of them were empty of people. "I hope things get better with your mother," Patrick said.

"Thank you," Ada said.

"If they don't, it's okay."

"I love her," Ada said. "I don't know why she doesn't feel it. I know she loves me too, but I can't feel it either."

As they walked farther into the city, the houses along the canal became more inhabited. They passed a building with wide bay windows. Inside it was set up like a stage, with lights shaded by big black hoods directed at one spot on the floor. They stopped to watch as a woman in a red dress stepped into the light. They heard the clicking of a camera, but the photographer was out of sight beside the window. She had blonde hair gathered at the neck, although some strands had been allowed to tumble loose down her back. The dress reminded Ada of a red flower, blooming just enough to reveal the furthest reaches of her body, pale ankles and delicate wrists. There was a low, plush sofa that she sat on, stretching out her feet in front of her. She wore high, pointed shoes, red satin with gold buckles. She laughed at something the photographer said, and her face collapsed into shadow as she turned her head away from the lights. Gold earrings hung from her soft, small ears.

"She looks like an angel," Patrick said.

The woman turned towards the window. Ada knew she had seen them. The face of the photographer appeared beside her. He was old, with a chipped tooth. He said something through the window, but they couldn't hear him. Holding a finger up to show that they should wait, he unlocked the clasp and pushed it open.

"Doesn't she look beautiful?" he said. "Like a goddess."

"We didn't mean to watch," Ada said.

"She's my wife," he said. "I take pictures of her because I want her to know how beautiful she is." Behind him, the woman laughed again. The undulations of her laugh reminded Ada of a small bird singing to a blue sky.

"Let them in," she said. "They're lovely." The man pushed the window open farther.

"Come in," he said. "You can see how I take the pictures."

They climbed over the low sill. The room was bigger than it had looked from the outside. Gauze curtains shifted in the breeze. In the corner stood a tripod with a camera.

The woman introduced herself as Jen. She offered the back of her tanned, wrinkled hand for them to kiss. The man was Giovanni. He wore a diamond stud in his ear. He asked them if they were a couple and neither of them knew what to say.

"It doesn't matter," he said. "Let me take your picture. You both look so gorgeous. So young."

He made them sit together on the couch. Ada took off her coat. Beneath it she had on a shirt and black jeans. Jen gave her a silver necklace to wear, and she gave Patrick a cap with a peaked tip that pushed his curly hair down across his forehead.

The pictures didn't take long. Giovanni told them not to smile.

"You're young," he said. "You should be serious. Fun is for when you get to our age."

After he'd taken the pictures, he showed them to Ada and Patrick. Ada didn't recognize the two people she saw staring back. Her face glowed as if it was lit from the inside. Patrick's sharp face beneath the black hat was somber and handsome. Both of them looked very young, more like siblings than lovers.

"I've never looked like that," she said.

"You look brilliant," Patrick said.

"I'll print you a copy," Giovanni said. "No charge."

They waited on the couch while he went into another room. Jen stood by the window. With the light behind her Ada saw that the delicate skin around her mouth was wrinkled.

"Gio loves to take pictures," she said.

Giovanni came back with a folder. Ada noticed that he had a black ribbon tied around his wrist.

"One for each of you," he said.

They thanked him and climbed back out through the window. He left it open behind them, and they heard the sound of happy laughter as they walked away.

When they were saying goodbye, Patrick seemed sad. Ada asked him what was wrong. He had walked her all the way home, and they were standing now in the lobby of her building.

"You don't like me," he said. "Not in the way that I like you."

"No," Ada said. "But I do like you." He took her hand and absentmindedly stroked her palm.

"I'm sorry about what your mother said." He turned her hand over and closed both of his around it. "You believe her," he said.

"Yes," Ada said.

"I don't know what to do about it," he said. "It seems like nothing I do will make any difference."

"I believe her," Ada said, "because she's right."

Patrick let go of her hand.

"I don't think so," he said. "But it's only what you think that matters."

When Ada arrived upstairs, she looked at the picture Giovanni had taken. The glow was still there, pouring out from her face as if the pores in her skin had been filled in with liquid gold.

THE NEXT DAY, Ada went back. She wanted to walk the same way she and Patrick had walked, along the canal, to see if Jen and Giovanni would still be there. Maybe she could talk to them about what was happening. She knew Patrick wouldn't come back to see her. The path was empty, and it felt like nobody else was left on Earth. She realized that she missed him. When he was with her, she existed.

When she passed the house, no lights were on, and the curtains were drawn. Disappointed, she continued on towards the city center. It was colder than it had been the last time, and the sky was gray.

The canal was traversed by a series of bridges. Trains ran along them, rumbling over Ada's head. To get through, she had to pass along narrow, dark passages, separated from the water by a single railing. Above her she could hear the sounds of pigeons roosting. Proximity to the water made her cold, and she buttoned up her coat. One particular bridge was longer than the others, and the passage was more of an alleyway, littered with bottles and polystyrene boxes stained with leftover food.

A flyer on the ground caught her attention. She picked it up. HELP WANTED, it said. There was a telephone number printed at the bottom.

She felt something. It was like a shiver that started at the base of her skull and ran downwards, disappearing into the ground. She dropped the flyer back on the muddy path. It was getting dark. Ada turned around and began the long walk home. There was a tugging sensation in her stomach. Since she had returned from Greece, she had been ignoring it, but the voice was still there, crying out to her for help. It harassed her, pulling at her, dragging her down to a dark place underfoot that she tried her best to pretend wasn't there.

When she reached the lobby of her building, she had an overwhelming feeling of relief. The light was warm and yellow. Although it was still early in the evening, nobody passed her as she went towards the elevator. She unbuttoned her coat but kept it on. When she got upstairs, she sat in the bathtub but didn't run the water. She hadn't turned the lights on, and the room was dark. She leaned her head against the lip and closed her eyes.

She was exhausted. There was an ache in her stomach, and she put both of her hands over it, as if she could smooth it away. The darkness of the bathroom was a relief. Her eyes felt like two glowing coals. There was a strange power in the feeling, as if she could see everything, as if her gaze could send whatever she looked at up in smoke. She felt mystical, or magical, filled with some inhuman force. Sitting in the bath with the cold enamel against her neck, she imagined everything around her burning up, a whole world collapsing into delicate, feathery flames. In the middle of the flames was a girl sitting in a chair before a white table. She had brown hair and pale skin with a reddish undertone, and she sat slightly slumped forwards, as if something was pressing down on her from behind. She wore a loose blue outfit that reminded Ada of the scrubs she'd seen worn by doctors and nurses. It looked too big for her, bunched around the shoulders. Ada looked down and saw that her feet were bare.

The girl looked at her. Ada took a step forwards. She had expected the girl's eyes to be dark and empty, but she saw that they were sparkling and alive despite her slumped posture.

The girl didn't say anything. She looked up at Ada from where she was sitting, with a blank expression on her face. Her face was unfamiliar, the face of a stranger, but Ada recognized it. She watched as it was eaten away by the flames.

The daydream was so vivid it disturbed her. Ada's phone was in her pocket. She called Patrick and asked him to come over.

He said that he would be there in an hour. She got out of the bath and went into the main room. Outside it was dark, but time had lost its meaning. Ada turned on the lamp beside her bed, and the whole apartment was suddenly filled with soft yellow light. She could almost feel it on her skin, like liquid warmth.

BEFORE HE ARRIVED, she changed her clothes. She put the clothes she had been wearing in the washing machine and turned it on. Then she washed her hands. When she was done, she went downstairs to the lobby to wait for him. She felt determined, as if something inside her had found a new equilibrium. In the corridor, waiting for the elevator, she was comforted by the softness of the carpet beneath her feet. Everything was finally still.

The elevator door opened, and standing before her was Atticus.

He stepped out.

"I've been down to the swimming pool every day, but I haven't seen you," he said. His voice was low, and he looked at her with a peculiar expression on his face, love mixed with sadness, as if he were admiring a beautiful coat that he had given away.

Ada stared at him. He looked old, even older than he had before. His eyes were ringed with red like those of a saggy-faced dog.

"How long have you been here?" she asked.

"A week," he said. "I'm staying at Neil's. I woke up one morning and I knew I had to come back."

Ada got into the elevator, leaving him behind her in the corridor. As she pressed the button for the ground floor, she noticed that her hands were shaking. When she got downstairs, she tried to refind the balance she had felt so acutely before the elevator doors had opened. Atticus's face loomed before her. She had almost forgotten what he looked like, although it had only been a few months since she'd last seen him. He was like a dream, or a ghost, something that had crossed the river that divided her thoughts from the world around her. He was older than her father, and she'd believed him when he said that he loved her, as if it was possible to love someone after meeting them twice. She remembered his rounded fingernails and the soft curls of his gray hair, and how scared he'd been to lose her when she had stepped in front of the car.

Patrick was on his way. Atticus was in the past. There was no place for him now. Entering the brightly lit lobby, she told herself she would forget about him. The clarity of the situation didn't erase her feeling that something special, something she couldn't quite remember, had been lost, like a gold coin dropped into the sea.

PATRICK ARRIVED WEARING a thick wool sweater. He'd had his hair cut and it stood up from his head in a choppy sea of short waves. When he saw her, he gave her a hug. His arms were warm, and his neck was smooth against her face.

"I'm so glad you called me," he said.

They took the elevator up in silence. Ada was afraid that Atticus would still be standing in the hallway, but he was gone. She wondered if he had actually been there, or if she had imagined it. Patrick followed her into her apartment. He sat on the bed rather than at the table. Ada sat next to him. She waited for him to take off his thick sweater, and then she kissed him. It was the first time she had kissed anyone. His mouth felt the same as before, warm and dry. There was stubble on his cheeks that scraped against her chin. He turned towards her and put one hand on her shoulder, the other on her elbow. When he turned back around and leaned down to take off his shoes, she said, "I do like you."

Afterwards, when they were naked again under the bedcovers, he asked her if she was okay.

"Why do you ask?"

"It's polite."

"It makes it sound like you think you've hurt me."

"I don't think that." He was picking at a loose thread in the duvet cover. "I didn't expect you to call," he said. Ada was imagining Atticus, sitting alone in his borrowed apartment. She wanted to ask him what had happened between them, to know if he understood any better than she did. Somehow, she knew what he would say—that they had loved and wanted each other, and still did. For him, that was all that their connection had been. Something about the simplicity made Ada angry, but she didn't understand what, for her, had made it more than that.

"I changed my mind," Ada said. Patrick didn't reply. Ada wondered if he didn't believe her, but she didn't know how to prove it beyond what had already happened. He was lying on his side, facing her. His brown eyes reflected the yellow lamplight. "What did you do today?" she asked him.

"I went to see a play," he said. "It was about two old people who live in a dustbin."

"I know that play," Ada said. He rolled onto his back and propped his head up on his arm. "I studied it at university." She remembered the professor who had taught it to her, a young Irish woman with curly blonde hair who always wore a brown turtleneck.

"I liked it," he said. "It was funny. I wish I could write something funny."

"I think most funny writing isn't intentional," she said. He smiled without looking at her.

"Not like funny people," he said.

Ada was sitting up, her bare back resting against the headboard. She pressed one of her feet against Patrick's side. He stroked it absentmindedly.

"Do you like me?" she asked him.

"Yes," he said.

Ada got up to go to the bathroom. She felt warm and happy. Her skin was flushed and her hair was tangled. She felt something wet on the back of her neck and put up her hand to feel it. Water ran over her fingertips, but she couldn't feel where it was coming from. It was warm. She called Patrick to the bathroom and asked him if he could see.

"There's nothing there," he said. "It's probably just sweat."

Ada dried it with a towel, and decided that he was right, but there was a cold wedge in her stomach, as if a draft was blowing in.

After he left, she slept badly. She woke up several times thinking it was the morning before the real sky grew light. As soon as dawn broke, she got up and went down to the swimming pool.

Atticus was there. His patterned towel was wrapped around his waist. He looked up when she came in, and smiled.

"The walls of your bedroom are green," she said. "Like seafoam."

ACKNOWLEDGMENTS

Thank you to, in no particular order, Jacqueline Ko, Jessica Bullock, Sarah Chalfant, Mo Crist, Cosmo Hinsman, Rachel Cusk, Jessye and Molly Clarke, Adrian Clarke, Siemon and Foiy Scamell-Katz, Henn Mossery-Golan, David Leavitt, Camille Bordas, Sheila Heti, Jasey Roberts, and Yolanda Kwadey.

A NOTE ON THE AUTHOR

ALBERTINE CLARKE is originally from London, although she is now based in Brooklyn, New York. *The Body Builders* is her first novel.